The Lady That Got Away

THE DARROW SISTERS
BOOK ONE

FIONA MIERS

THE LADY THAT GOT AWAY

First edition. April 30, 2024.

Copyright © 2024 Harley Romance Publishing.

Contact: harleyromancepublishing@gmail.com

Website: www.harleyromancepublishing.com

Written by Fiona Miers

Chapter One

Lady Eleanor fixed her gaze on the rain-soaked gardens of her family's London residence. Unfortunately, the dull gray sky matched the somber atmosphere in her home. Ever since her father's passing, a cloud of sadness enveloped the house. Dark and always lonely, despite the rest of the family living in it.

After enduring six long months of his absence, the burden of her responsibilities only seemed to intensify with each passing day. With her mother still entrenched in mourning, managing the estate fell on her shoulders. Eleanor didn't know what it felt like to love someone else to so much that life without them seemed impossible, and from the evidence laid out before her, she hoped she never would. The pain of losing that love seemed too much to bear, even for someone as aloof as her mother.

As she contemplated the bleak future that lay ahead, a soft knock on the door drew her attention away from the dreary view. Her heart quickened with anticipation. Who would call on her in such inclement weather?

"Enter." To her surprise, her voice remained steady despite the turmoil happening inside her mind.

The door swung open, and Olivia, her sister, stepped into the room holding an enormous bouquet of roses. The crimson petals contrasted with the gray surroundings, and Eleanor grinned at their beauty. A delicate ribbon tied the stems, its color a perfect match to the roses. An attached note was folded so she couldn't read the message.

"For you." Olivia gave her a soft smile and presented the bouquet.

They'd had no choice but to let most of their servants go three months after Father died. The only one they could afford to keep was Maribel, the cook. Eleanor hated that her sisters were forced to do menial work, but they had few options at this stage.

Eleanor took the flowers, her fingers trembling as she gazed at the exquisite blooms. "They're beautiful."

She could hardly believe her eyes. Who could have sent her such a thoughtful and extravagant gift? And at exactly the time she needed her spirits lifted.

Olivia stared at Eleanor with wide, questioning eyes. "Who are they from, sister? Tell me."

Eleanor untied the ribbon and carefully unfolded the note. The elegant handwriting was familiar, and her heart skipped a beat as she read the words.

My dearest Eleanor,

Amid life's storms, may these roses remind you of the beauty that endures even in the darkest of times. You are not alone in your grief and responsibilities. Lean on those who care for you, and together, we shall weather any tempest that may come your way.

Yours always,

Satterfield

"They're from Lord Satterfield." Eleanor leaned forward to take in the bouquet's scent. Lord Satterfield had been a close friend of her father's and a man she'd known since childhood. He had always been kind to them, but this gesture touched her deeply. The roses, so full of life and color, were a symbol of hope amidst the darkness.

"That was very nice of him." Olivia's words may have been polite, but her voice held nothing but suspicion.

Eleanor ignored her sister's tone and clutched the bouquet to her chest. For a moment, the weight lifted from her shoulders and a glimmer of warmth filled her heart. She wasn't alone, not really. With family friends like Lord Satterfield by her side, she could face whatever challenges lay ahead.

"Yes, it was." Eleanor let out a sigh. "These will be perfect in the foyer, don't you think?"

Olivia nodded. "Perhaps if mother sees them, she will smile."

"Perhaps."

The chance that her mother would leave her room, let alone pass by these flowers, was as slight as the sun chasing away the clouds in the middle of winter. But Eleanor carried the flowers down the hallway for Olivia to find a vase and place them on the small foyer table.

Eleanor had avoided her estate management responsibilities for some time, but she couldn't continue to do so. With another sigh, she headed to her father's study—her study now.

Soon, the many facets of managing her family's estate occupied her thoughts. Olivia had returned to the schoolroom, and her three younger sisters were engaged in their lessons nearby. Their daily lessons and bright chatter provided the appearance of normalcy during the family's time of grieving. As she reviewed the financial ledgers, the door creaked open. Her youngest sister, Mary, peeked in with a mischievous glint in her eyes.

"Ellie." Mary used the childhood nickname only she could use. "A gentleman is here to see you."

Eleanor frowned at her baby sister. That was strange. "A gentleman? Who is it?"

Mary's grin widened. "It's Lord Weston."

Her stomach twisted at the mere mention of that name. Alexander Weston was a notorious rake in town. He was a man known for his scandalous behavior and many affairs with London's most sought-after ladies—especially of the married variety. He was not the type of visitor she expected, nor did she desire his company.

She set aside the ledger, trying to maintain her composure in the face of such news. "Lord Weston? What could he want with me?"

Mary's eyes sparkled with curiosity. "He wouldn't say, but he insisted it was a matter of utmost importance."

Eleanor blew out a loud sigh. Rejecting him without a reason would be folly, especially given it was an appropriate time for receiving visitors, and Mary had informed him she was in. Lord Weston's reputation was notorious, and his presence in their home was bound to raise eyebrows in the household and among the neighbors. But now that he was here, she couldn't send him away either, not without knowing what had brought him here.

"Very well." She stiffened her shoulders and swallowed. Her voice was still steady. She sounded mostly normal, considering how tight her throat had become. "Please show him into the drawing room."

Mary darted out of the study, leaving Eleanor alone with her thoughts. She straightened her posture, left the safety of the study, and made her way to the drawing room, determined to handle this unexpected visit with grace and poise, no matter what Lord Weston might desire.

Curiosity gnawed at her as she walked into the drawing room. What on earth could he want after all these years?

Moments after she sat, the door opened once more, and Weston strolled in with an air of effortless confidence. He was even more handsome than she'd remembered.

He wore his dark hair tousled in an artful disarray, and his attire, while fashionable, carried a hint of the rakish charm he was known for. The whispered gasps from her sisters, who had escaped from the schoolroom and were peeking from the corner, were a little embarrassing as they beheld the notorious visitor.

"My dear Lady Eleanor." His keen, steel-grey eyes, sharp and discerning, twinkled with a hint of roguish charm, and his lips bore a slight, knowing smile. "I trust you are well?"

The cad had the nerve to address her so casually, as if they were old friends after everything he'd done. Eleanor nodded as politely as custom dictated and not one iota more, her composure intact despite the disconcerting presence of the charming rogue before her. "As well as one can be under the circumstances, Lord Weston. What brings you here?"

He offered a gracious bow. "A matter of great importance, my lady. One that requires your keen insight and discretion."

Eleanor raised an eyebrow, intrigued now. "Pray, enlighten me, Lord Weston."

He stepped closer, his voice lowering to a conspiratorial tone. "It concerns a certain scandal, my dear lady. A matter that could prove disastrous if it were to come to light."

Eleanor's curiosity deepened, and she leaned forward, her interest piqued. "Go on."

Lord Weston paused, his gaze holding hers with an intensity that sent a shiver down her spine. "I believe your family has been unfairly maligned in recent gossip columns, and I offer my help in quelling the baseless rumors."

Eleanor blinked, taken aback by the unexpected turn of events. She'd thought that Lord Weston would be here to speak of a scandal he was associated with, not the other way around.

Her family's reputation was, indeed, important to her, and the recent rumors of her father's debts, her mother's lapse in fortitude, and how she and her sisters were on the precipice of falling from grace had been a great upset that kept her awake at night.

However, she couldn't help but remain cautious of Lord Weston's motives.

"Why would you be willing to assist with such a matter?" she asked.

He gave her a charming smile, his eyes glinting with a hint of sincerity. "Because, my lady, I believe that a sense of honor can move even notorious rakes. And because I admire the strength and determination you have shown in these trying times."

Her heart pounded as anger rose within her.

"Why don't I believe you?" She arched her brow.

Lord Weston's smile didn't waver as he met her skeptical gaze. "I understand your doubts, Lady Eleanor." His smooth tone grated rather than calmed. "But I assure you, my intentions are genuine. My reputation may be that of a rogue, but there is more to me than meets the eye."

She doubted that. She'd already seen firsthand how untrustworthy the nobleman before her could be. But she couldn't deny that they needed help. Her family's honor hung in the balance, and if he could help restore it, she should consider his offer seriously.

The memories of their tumultuous past came to the forefront of her thoughts. Lady Abigail's betrayal with Weston had left a lasting scar on her heart. She had never spoken to Abigail again, but she confronted Lord Weston about the affair in a heated argument. Their relationship had soured irreparably. How could she forgive him for the humiliation and heartache he had caused? Could she ever forgive him, no matter how much time passed, or how grim her circumstances?

"Why should I believe you?" Her voice carried more than a trace of bitterness.

Lord Weston's gaze bored into hers. If he was looking for a flicker of trust, then he was heading for disappointment. But his reply was earnest. "Because I care. I always have."

A beat of silence passed, then he added, "I admired your father."

"Oh, please–"

He took a step towards her. "It is the truth," he insisted. "I have been away these past months, traveling the countryside with my grandmother. I heard news of his passing while I was in Devonshire, and I sent you a note with flowers." He glanced at the new vase of roses, narrowing his eyes at the flowers that were not from him, then he looked back at her. "Did you get them?"

She had.

And she'd thrown them away.

It had been petty of her, because the gesture had been polite. But she didn't want sympathy. Not from him. If anything, she wanted him to return to his usual arrogance. Make a rude or obnoxious comment. That was familiar to her. This man in front of her looked like Lord Alexander Weston, but he didn't act like him, and that set of more than a few alarm bells in her head. If anyone knew how to be a wolf in sheep's clothing, it was him.

"While I appreciate…whatever this is." She stood. "I can take care of my family perfectly well with no outside intervention."

His eyes narrowed. "I know you can, but that doesn't mean you have to".

She jammed her arms across her chest, a most unladylike gesture. "Speak plainly, Lord Weston."

He glanced away. His jaw ticked, though she didn't understand why. Was he frustrated with her? She had done nothing wrong.

"I'm saying, if you could put that annoying pride aside—"

"Pride?" she snapped out the words. "You think I have pride?"

"Your pride gets in the way of your common sense," he snapped back. "I am just trying to help—"

"We have not requested your help." She walked toward him. "I don't want, nor do I need your help. And if this is some paltry way of honoring my father now that he succumbed to his illness, I relieve you of the burden. You do not need to do anything for us. We don't want it. *I* don't want it."

His gaze darkened. "You've never allowed me leave to explain what happened with Lady Abigail—"

She jerked back as if he had slapped her. "Don't speak her name. I will not listen to you saying her name."

"It is not just you who is suffering, you know. I'm here because I want to help. Because life is too short for petty misunderstandings. No one else visits or offers any assistance, do they?"

Her lips curved. "That's where you're wrong. Lord Satterfield—"

Lord Weston rolled his eyes. "Satterfield has wanted to marry you since your debut. Your father refused several times because he well knew that Satterfield is an old man full of nothing but ill intent."

Eleanor opened her mouth to respond but couldn't think of anything intelligent to say.

"Your father died with neither sons nor close male relatives, so the burden of finding a husband or a protector for you and your sisters falls on your mother." Alexander paced. "But she's too lost in mourning, so that burden has fallen to you. That is wrong. You should have your own time to grieve. And yet, if no one steps up help, what will happen? Do you want to keep firing staff and selling your jewelry until you are so bereft, not a soul—"

"I am very aware of the challenges my family faces." Her jaw tensed.

She was not pleased with his familiarity of their situation. "What I don't understand is why you're here."

"As I've said..." He flashed her a grin that, in the past, would have made her weak at the knees. "I'm here to help."

His charisma was undeniable, captivating all who crossed his path with his elegance and magnetic allure. Eleanor could not let herself succumb to it. She folded her hands in front of her. "And what do you suggest, since you seem to think you know everything?"

His grin widened. "That you marry me, of course."

Chapter Two

Alexander savored the shock that registered on Eleanor's face as his audacious proposal hung in the air. She'd never been pretty in the conventional sense, but in the faded drawing room, she stood with an effortless grace that commanded attention. Her dark hair, glossy as a raven's wing, was styled in elegant curls that framed her face and cascaded down her shoulders. He was used to seeing it adorned with pearls or ribbons that matched her gowns, but out of respect for her father, she wore no embellishments today.

Her piercing blue eyes, reminiscent of a clear winter sky, widened, and her lips parted in astonishment. He had expected her to be taken aback, but her reaction was even more delightful than he expected.

"M-m- marry you?" she sputtered, her tone incredulous. "You must be jesting, Lord Weston."

He chuckled to himself, appreciating the strength of her spirit. "I assure you, Eleanor, I'm quite serious."

Any other woman, especially one in her position, would fall over herself to accept his proposal. But not Eleanor.

Her initial astonishment soon transformed into a mixture of confusion and disbelief as evident by the myriad of emotions that crossed her beautiful face. She was struggling to comprehend the logic behind his suggestion.

"Do not address me as if we are friends. Why would you make such an offer?" Eleanor's tone was heavy with suspicion. "What would you gain from marrying me?"

Many things, some of which a lady like her would not like to hear.

He focused on the obvious. "It would solve both of our problems, Lady Eleanor. You need a protector and a way to secure your family's place in society. And I need a wife to mend my own tarnished reputation. It is an excellent solution, don't you think?"

He could almost see the wheels turning in her mind, the internal struggle between her natural wariness of him and the genuine need to safeguard her family's honor. She was a lady of intelligence and determination, and he admired those qualities.

Eleanor regarded him with uncertainty. "What assurance can you provide that this marriage would be more than a charade?"

He leaned in closer, his voice dropping to a low, intimate whisper. "In matters of the heart, I am deadly serious."

His proposal was daring, and it was also a gamble. He was offering more than just an alliance to protect their reputations. He was suggesting a marriage that would alter the course of their lives. Now, he awaited Eleanor's response, curious to see if she would accept his bold offer or dismiss it as mere folly.

"Are you..." She swallowed twice. "Are you laughing at me?" She tilted her head to the side, narrowing her eyes at him.

"Pardon me?" That wasn't what he'd expected her to say. "Laughing?"

"I could never marry you." She reached up to pat her perfect hair. He knew her well enough to know that touching her hair was a nervous gesture. "You're...you're..."

"Handsome? Charming? Deliriously wealthy?"

"You're a rake!" She paced the small room, any pretense of acting like the prim and proper lady vanished. This was the real Eleanor he knew. Wild. Audacious. Passionate. She couldn't contain the fire in her veins as she marched up and down the length of the room, and he couldn't take his eyes off her.

Her accusations about his rakish reputation made him chuckle. He had expected her to react strongly, given their shared history and her deep-seated distrust of him.

"I'm a what?" He feigned innocence as he observed her pacing the room.

Eleanor halted her restless steps and fixed him with a withering glare. "You are a notorious rake, Lord Weston, known for your scandalous affairs and reckless behavior. Marrying you would be a total disaster."

Alexander gave a sigh full of melodrama and stepped closer to her, his voice laced with mock sincerity. "Lady Eleanor, you wound me with your harsh judgments. But let me remind you that sometimes it takes a reformed rake to appreciate the true depth of love and commitment."

Eleanor's skepticism was clear, but she didn't deny his interesting argument. He was more than willing to shed his rakish image, and he needed to convince her of his sincerity.

He continued, his tone earnest, "I may have been a rogue, but I am offering you a chance to secure your family's future and protect their reputation. My wealth and resources can help you weather the storm of these rumors, Eleanor."

As he awaited her response, Alexander hoped with an earnestness that surprised him that she would direct the passion he saw in her eyes at the possibility of a future they could create together.

A future that transcended their tumultuous history.

"It's not about your wealth and resources." She stopped her pacing to face him. "I just don't trust you."

That gave him pause.

"Trust me?" He lifted his brow. "You don't need to trust me to marry me."

She blinked at him as though he were the one who had lost his mind. "Yes, I do. Even if the marriage is a farce, I would need to trust you not to—"

"To what?"

She looked away. "Make a fool of me."

His frustration was creeping in now. She was not the sort to play games, but it felt as though she were stringing him along instead of speaking her mind.

"I'm sorry, my lady, I do not understand what you mean," Alexander said.

She snorted, an unbecoming sound for a lady of her status, but one that turned his lips up into an amused smile.

"Oh, come on, Alexander." She fisted her hands on her hips. "Even if the marriage were in name only, I would not tolerate you seeing other women or blatantly keeping a mistress. You have a reputation of being free with yourself. I could never ask you to change your ways, and I wouldn't expect you to. But that does not mean I will tolerate your infidelity, even if it is a common occurrence amongst men of our social stature."

Her nose wrinkled with distaste, and Alexander regarded her with a mix of astonishment and admiration. Her straightforward declaration, despite the intricacies of their situation, held a stark honesty that he found both refreshing and challenging. Eleanor had always been fiercely independent and steadfast in her principles, and she was making it clear what she expected.

He took a moment to compose himself before responding, his amusement giving way to a more serious tone. "I see your point, Lady Eleanor. I understand your concerns, and I am willing to ensure your comfort and peace of mind in this arrangement. It's a small price to pay for the honor of having you by my side."

She gave him a long look. "What do you mean? Spell it out for me."

He took a step forward, repaying her honesty with a taste of his own. "I'm telling you, I would cease any dalliances with other women I might have otherwise continued. I promise I will not so much as flirt with the married women who chase me. You will find me a changed man if it means securing your hand. I told you I am reformed. It would not be difficult."

Eleanor jerked her head back. "I don't believe you."

He furrowed his brows. "Whyever not?"

"You're telling me you would marry me, even if we never...never even kissed." A delightful shade of pink touched her cheeks.

What else might make her blush as prettily? How far did that delightful blush extend?

She got herself under control. "If we never had intimate relations with anyone else?"

The tension in the room was palpable, and Alexander felt the weight of their unresolved issues pressing on him. He had hoped for their encounter to go more smoothly, but Eleanor's unwavering skepticism and resolute attitude were proving to be formidable barriers.

Alexander opened his mouth, ready to explain his intentions, but Eleanor cut him off before he could utter a word. "I do not believe you."

"I protest. You didn't let me answer." He raked his hand through his dark, thick hair.

Eleanor's eyes narrowed as she leveled a challenging stare at him. "I already know whatever comes out of your mouth will be a lie."

Her cynicism stung, and Alexander struggled to find the right words to bridge the gap between them. He had hoped to show her he was different now, that his intentions were genuine, but the wall she had built around herself seemed impenetrable.

"Ah. I forgot you know everything," he quipped, but his attempt at lightening the mood fell flat.

Eleanor was not in the mood for humor. "I knew about you and Abigail, and you denied it."

The mention of Abigail's name made Alexander's jaw clench. "I never—"

"I do not believe you," she interrupted, her voice unwavering.

The frustration in him boiled over, and he blurted out his exasperation, "You are infuriating, woman! I've come prepared to help you."

"I did not ask for your help." She faced him with a high chin and her shoulders back.

They stood locked in a battle of wills, their history and present situation colliding in a whirlwind of emotions. The path toward a resolution appeared fraught with obstacles, and convincing her of his sincerity would be a formidable challenge.

Alexander regarded Eleanor, his skepticism giving way to curiosity.

Her defiance was clear, but how on earth did she intend to navigate the perilous situation in which her family found itself?

"In fact…" She kept her chin high. "I don't need your help."

The fire in her eyes and her indefatigable determination were admirable, and it sparked a newfound respect within him. "You don't? Then what's your plan?"

Eleanor's gaze didn't waver as she responded with unshakable resolve. "I have a plan, Lord Weston, and it does not involve you. Be assured, I will safeguard my family's honor."

The declaration hung heavily in the air between them. She was proving to be a more formidable adversary than he had expected. Alexander couldn't help but admire her strength, even if it meant they were now on opposing sides of this precarious situation.

"Tell me." He shouldn't care. He should let it be. Her stubbornness was infuriating, and he needed to mind his own temper, since she seemed to be the only person who ever riled him to the same extent. "Does it involve Satterfield?"

Eleanor's expression remained unreadable for a moment, then her gaze flickered with a hint of surprise at his question. After a few seconds she offered a measured response. "It involves Lord Satterfield, but not in the way you might think."

Alexander leaned in closer, eager to understand the complexity of her situation. "And how does it involve him, Eleanor?"

She met his gaze with a mixture of defiance and vulnerability. "He is a trusted family friend, and he has offered support during this difficult time. However, our relationship is platonic, and I intend to keep it that way."

Alexander nodded, taking in her words and the unspoken subtext. Eleanor was determined to handle her family's predicament on her own terms, without relying on romantic entanglements, even with someone like Satterfield. While her independence was commendable, it also added another layer of complexity to their intricate situation.

Right now, wasn't the time to sow their fresh path of trust, but in time, he would show her his true nature.

He would also show her that she could not trust Satterfield. Not with her own, nor her family's honor.

Chapter Three

After Lord Weston's departure, the drawing room felt unnaturally silent, the air thick with the weight of his proposal and Eleanor's tumultuous thoughts. She found herself replaying their conversation, his words "a rescue" echoing mockingly in the quiet. It wasn't just the audacity of his proposal that troubled her but also the insinuation that she or her family needed rescuing—and from him, of all people.

Her younger sisters, Olivia, Caroline, and Mary had been studying in the adjacent room. Now they entered the drawing room, curiosity etched on their youthful faces.

"Ellie." Olivia widened her hazel eyes. "What happened? What did Lord Weston want?"

Their entrance broke the spell of Eleanor's ruminations, drawing her back to the immediate challenge of framing the situation in a way that would shield them from the harsher realities of their predicament. Involving her sisters in the family's struggles and secrets was unavoidable, but Eleanor had hoped to shield them from such concerns a little while longer.

Olivia's question, filled with innocence and worry, forced Eleanor to tread carefully. The responsibility of preserving their family's dignity while navigating these treacherous social waters fell heavily on her shoulders. She crafted her response to include them in the situation without overwhelming them.

"Lord Weston was here to discuss a proposal." Eleanor chose her words carefully. "Our family has been facing some difficulties in society, and he offered to help us navigate them."

She didn't want to admit to her sisters that she'd flatly refused his help. That would mean explaining their past, and she wasn't ready to do that.

Caroline, the vivacious and inquisitive sister, chimed in. "A proposal? What kind of proposal?"

Eleanor hesitated, struggling to find a way to explain the situation without revealing all. "It is a delicate matter. Lord Weston suggested that he and I might enter a partnership of sorts, to protect our family's reputation."

Mary, the youngest, seemed to sense the gravity of the situation. Her big, innocent eyes grew even larger as she asked, "A partnership? Does that mean you are getting married, Eleanor?"

Eleanor's heart ached as she considered the implications for her sisters. Her decision would impact their lives as well. "Not exactly, Mary. It's a complicated situation, and there are many things to consider. We will not be rushing into anything."

Quite the opposite, in fact.

Olivia and Caroline exchanged knowing glances, and it was clear that they were not satisfied with the vague explanation. But she couldn't bring herself to reveal the fact that she'd rejected Lord Weston and why. She wanted to protect her family, but she also wanted to shield her sisters from the harsh realities of the world outside their sheltered existence.

Mary's frown deepened. "Eleanor, Mama has been in bed all day. She didn't even take her morning walk. I fear she's getting worse. Could this partnership help her too?"

Their mother's worsening condition added another layer of urgency to Eleanor's considerations. She reached out and gently held Mary's hand, trying to comfort her. "If I do decide to enter it, Mary, I hope it will." The possibility that this unwanted partnership could offer some relief was a bitter pill, sweetened only by the hope of aiding their beloved mother. "The suggested partnership is intended to help the entire family, including Mama."

Caroline and Olivia, who had been exchanging knowing glances, now voiced their concerns as well. "Ellie, we trust your judgment," Caroline said, "but we're just worried about what this means for all of us."

Olivia nodded in agreement, her eyes filled with a mixture of understanding and anxiety. "We want to support you, but we also want to know you are making the right decisions."

Eleanor had to tread carefully, as the weight of their family's future rested heavily on her shoulders. She squeezed Mary's hand. "I promise I will keep you all informed as this situation unfolds. We will face it together as a family, just as we always have. We will do whatever it takes to protect Mama and ensure a better future for all of us."

Even if that meant going on bended knee to her father's friend.

Caroline asked, "Ellie, are you going to agree to Lord Weston's proposal, then?"

There was no way she could do that. But instead of telling her sisters the truth, she offered a soft, reassuring smile. "Caroline, I am exploring our options to find the one that suits us best. We will not rush into anything, and we will make the decision that is in the best interest of our family. Your support means the world to me, though. Thank you."

Olivia nodded in agreement. "We are here for you, Ellie. We trust your judgment, and we know you will do what is best for all of us."

Eleanor felt a swell of gratitude for her sisters' unwavering support and comfort. Somehow, she would find a way to protect their family.

"Eleanor," Olivia began hesitantly, "The beautiful bouquet of roses in the drawing room from Lord Satterfield—what do they mean?"

Eleanor's thoughts were momentarily diverted from Lord Weston when Olivia brought up the unexpected delivery that had arrived earlier in the day—a bouquet of roses so vibrant, they seemed almost defiant in the face of their sombre mood. The flowers stood out like a beacon of warmth in the house.

Eleanor took a moment to consider her response. Her sisters were inquisitive, and keeping secrets within the family was not always easy. With a sigh, she decided to be honest. "Lord Satterfield is a dear friend of our family, and he has been a great source of support since Father's passing. The roses were a gesture of kindness and comfort for all of us."

Olivia glanced at her younger sisters before leaning a little closer to Eleanor, her voice low, as if aware of the delicate territory she was navigating. "I meant, why did Lord Satterfield send flowers, and red roses especially, personally addressed to you? Just out of kindness?"

Caroline and Mary listened intently, and Caroline added, "He must care about you a great deal to send such beautiful flowers, Ellie."

Eleanor paused, her mind racing through the implications of Olivia's question. To the world, Lord Satterfield was a friend of her father and the family, respected and admired for his benevolence and integrity. Yet, the roses suggested a personal connection, a gesture of support that went beyond mere acquaintance.

Caroline's remark about Lord Satterfield's evident care opened a floodgate of emotions within Eleanor. Yes, he cared, perhaps more deeply than they all realized. His actions, always subtle and discreet, had been a constant throughout her life.

The moment was ripe with unspoken questions and the weight of decisions yet to be made. Eleanor appreciated Lord Satterfield's support, yet she was acutely aware of the complexities that their friendship entailed, especially now, as their family faced potential ruin.

"He has been very supportive." Eleanor chose her words with care. "The roses? They're a gesture of comfort, nothing more."

Her attempt to downplay the significance of the gift didn't go unnoticed by her sisters, whose exchanged glances spoke volumes of their unsaid thoughts.

Red roses from Lord Satterfield and a marriage proposal from Lord Weston. What a day this had been.

Eleanor's neck prickled. She turned to catch Olivia gazing at her with a thoughtful expression, as if she wanted to ask a question but wasn't sure how.

The girl had always been perceptive. Eleanor turned to her. "You may ask me anything, Olivia."

Olivia nodded. "I have noticed that you and Lord Weston do not seem to get along very well. Why is that?"

Eleanor shifted uncomfortably in her seat, her eyes briefly avoiding her sister's gaze. She had never discussed the complex history she shared with Lord Weston, and she certainly didn't want to delve into the depths of their turbulent relationship in front of her younger sisters.

"There have been misunderstandings between us," Eleanor replied vaguely, choosing her words carefully.

Olivia nodded and didn't press her further, for which Eleanor was grateful. But she was aware that in the future, she might not be so lucky.

Caroline tried to lighten the mood. "Well, whatever happened between you two, I hope you can put it behind you for the sake of this partnership, Ellie."

Eleanor offered a reassuring smile, grateful for her sisters' understanding. "I still do not know if I will accept his proposal. But regardless of my final choice, we are all committed to making the best of the situation, for Mama and for each other. That is what matters most."

Mary gripped Eleanor's skirt. "If Lord Weston's proposal would help us, why won't you accept it?"

Eleanor paused, her gaze shifting from Mary to Olivia to Caroline. It was time to explain her reservations, especially to Mary, who was still learning the intricacies of the world in which they lived.

Caroline added softly, "Mary is right. Lord Weston's offer might be a lifeline for us. Why are you so hesitant?"

Eleanor took a deep breath. "I appreciate Lord Weston's willingness to assist, but I do not want to be obligated to anyone, especially not him. You see, Mary, sometimes accepting help can come with strings attached, and it may lead to a loss of our independence and the ability to make our own choices. I want to ensure that whatever path we take, it is on our terms, without sacrificing our family's integrity."

"I have heard that Lord Weston is more than fair," Caroline said. "My friend told me that her sister knows Lord Weston personally, and that he helped her with a financial burden without asking for anything in return. Is what you're concerned about true?"

Eleanor's expression turned somber. "Lord Weston may be charitable on occasions, but I have had my own experiences with him in the past, and I will not fall for his false promises again. I want what's best for our family, but it is necessary to maintain our dignity. I also don't want him to hold anything over me, a weapon he can use against me when I am at my most vulnerable."

"You? Vulnerable?" Olivia rolled her eyes. "Please tell me the day you let down your guard, Ellie. I'm sure you would be a sight to behold."

Mary tugged at Eleanor's skirt again. "If you do not accept Lord Weston's assistance, what do you plan to do?"

Eleanor sighed, her shoulders slumping with the weight of their uncertain future. It was a question that had been plaguing her thoughts as well. "I wish I had a clear answer, Mary, but I am not entirely sure. All I know is that something must be done to protect our family's reputation. We will explore all options and find a way forward, together."

The sisters shared a solemn moment, the gravity of their situation settling over the group. Mary tugged at the end of her braid, while Olivia smoothed the wrinkles from the blue dress from last season that she wore.

"I just want to go back to the way things were before," Caroline muttered, more to herself than to anyone as she picked up her sewing. "I wish Father was here."

Eleanor's heart clenched. She did too, more than anything.

Her sisters continued to talk, but Eleanor remained silent. She was focused on their main question—what did she plan to do? The truth was, she didn't know. But Lord Weston's offer had made her realize one thing. The best way to save her family would be to marry someone wealthy. And if it wasn't Lord Alexander Weston who'd offered himself up, she'd be prepared to do just that.

Chapter Four

As Weston exited Eleanor's residence, his frustration simmered, an unwelcome companion in the cool air. He had naively anticipated a different reception, one marked by openness rather than the stark rejection he received. The sting of Eleanor's refusal gnawed at him, a visceral reminder of his miscalculations and the chasm between their current standing.

Mounting the steps to his waiting carriage, a sleek embodiment of his status, Alexander moved with a distracted grace, his mind ensnared by the day's events.

The door closed with a thud, and he slumped back into the comfortable leather, alone with nothing but his turbulent thoughts for company.

The carriage began its journey home, the rhythmic cadence of hooves against cobblestones serving as a backdrop to his brooding. The drive home offered no respite, as Eleanor's fierce independence and unyielding spirit occupied his thoughts. He had come here with the intention of assisting her and her family, but she had resisted him at every turn.

Despite the sting of her rebuff, he couldn't help but admire her resolve, even as it clashed with his intentions. It was this very tenacity that intrigued him, challenging his perceptions, igniting a stubborn flame of respect.

As the manor faded into the distance, he found himself torn between irritation and understanding. He admired Eleanor's tenacity and her determination to maintain her family's dignity, but it also frustrated him that she was so obstinate. He had never encountered such resistance before, and it irked him to no end.

The passing cityscape, with its blur of lights and shadows, mirrored his tumultuous thoughts. Eleanor's scathing reference to him as a rake reverberated in his mind, a stark echo of their shared past and the complexity of their previous entanglement.

The carriage jolted over a particularly rough patch of road, and he was jolted from his reverie. He ran a hand through his hair, feeling the weight of his responsibilities pressing upon him. Helping Eleanor's family was not merely a whim on his part, it was a matter of principle. A sense of duty to rectify the wrongs he had committed in the past.

His estate loomed into view, a sprawling manor nestled amid lush greenery. As the carriage pulled up to the front entrance, he couldn't shake the regret that he had failed in his mission. Eleanor's rejection was a bitter pill to swallow, but it only fueled his determination to find a way to assist her family, whether she accepted his help or not.

He stepped out of the carriage, his mind already formulating new plans and strategies. He had been called many things in his life—rake, scoundrel, rogue—but he would not let Eleanor's rejection deter him from helping her. He would find a way to aid her family, to prove that he was more than just the reputation that had preceded him.

He stepped into the grand foyer of his imposing townhouse. The entrance hall exuded opulence, with its polished marble floors and soaring ceilings adorned with intricate molding. The walls were draped in luxurious fabrics, and glistening crystal chandeliers bathed the space in a warm, golden glow.

As he crossed the threshold, the butler, Bronson, greeted him with a respectful nod. "Welcome home, my lord," Bronson said, his voice a model of deference. "May I assist you in any way?"

"I will get a whiskey in my study."

Bronson nodded once. "As you wish."

Alexander's path led him through a lavishly decorated hallway, adorned with antique oil paintings and finely crafted furniture. A servant approached, extending a stack of correspondence for his review, but Alexander brushed it aside with a distracted gesture. He had no interest in the mundane details of daily life, not when there were far more pressing matters at hand.

The servant retreated with a bow, and Alexander moved through a set of imposing double doors into his private study. His study, a haven of leather-bound wisdom and mahogany resilience, offered a semblance of comfort, yet the solitude it provided was a stark contrast to the warmth of genuine connection he sought to reestablish with Eleanor.

As he settled into his high-backed leather chair, Alexander leaned back, his thoughts once again drifting to Eleanor. Her words of rejection haunted him as he pondered his next move. It was an unfamiliar sensation for him, a man who was accustomed to getting what he wanted.

But as he looked around his luxurious study, he couldn't escape the emptiness that lingered. His life had been defined by pleasure and indulgence, but Eleanor's situation offered him a chance at something more profound—a chance to right the wrongs of his past.

His mission to assist the young woman and her family was far from over. This rejection was just the beginning of a complex dance between them, a dance that he was determined to see through to its conclusion. Eleanor's rebuff served not as a deterrent but as a catalyst, propelling him toward a resolution to bridge the divide irrespective of her initial resistance.

It didn't help that Satterfield was involved.

The involvement of the man, a detail that should have been inconsequential, gnawed at him with unexpected intensity. This wasn't merely about offering aid, it was a battle for influence. For a meaningful presence in Eleanor's life. The notion of rivalry, of competing for a role in Eleanor's future, sparked a blend of irritation and intrigue—a challenge to his accustomed dominance.

His mind was a whirlwind of thoughts, a relentless storm that showed no signs of abating. It was not like him to be so affected by the actions of others, and yet he found himself grappling with emotions he had never experienced.

Satterfield's involvement in Eleanor's life annoyed him. He couldn't help but contemplate the man's motives. What was his true purpose in offering support to Eleanor and her family? Was it genuine concern for their well-being, or did he have other, more self-serving intentions?

As he delved into this tangled web of thoughts, a surprising emotion washed over Alexander—jealousy. It was an unfamiliar sensation, one he had seldom encountered. He prided himself on his ability to remain detached and emotionally uninvolved, but the prospect of another man making inroads into Eleanor's life—and her bed—stirred something within him. The implications of Eleanor's potential closeness to Satterfield ignited a fervor to assert his worth, not merely as a suitor but as a genuine ally.

He couldn't deny that Eleanor and Satterfield had a history, a friendship that had existed long before he'd entered the picture. It was a history that made him question his own place in Eleanor's life. The thought of her confiding in Satterfield, seeking his counsel, made a pang of jealousy coil in his chest.

Alexander couldn't quite fathom the depth of his reaction. He found himself in uncharted territory, in a position where he had to compete for Eleanor's trust and affection, something that both vexed and intrigued him.

He ran a hand through his disheveled hair, his mind racing with conflicting emotions. He had never been a man to back down from a challenge, and Eleanor had just unwittingly presented him with one.

With a determined clench of his jaw, Alexander decided that if Satterfield was to be a player in this complex dance, he would not be outdone. He would prove himself a more valuable and steadfast associate to Eleanor and her family. He would ensure his motives were beyond reproach, his intentions crystal clear. Jealousy would be a driving force, but so would his newfound determination to see this through to its conclusion.

As he contemplated his next moves, Alexander acknowledged that the journey he had embarked on was now far more intricate and perilous than he had first imagined. But he was willing to embrace the challenge.

The shadows of the past and the specter of rivalry loomed large, yet they also illuminated a path toward personal growth and redemption.

"Time to act," he murmured to himself, the resolve in his voice carving clarity from the chaos of his thoughts. The journey ahead promised no easy victories, but Alexander was no stranger to adversity. If anything, Eleanor's defiance had rekindled a determination to rise above the fray, to transform the complexities of their connection into a testament of enduring resolve and heartfelt reparation.

Alexander sat at his mahogany desk, a stack of letters and documents spread out before him. His study was bathed in the soft glow of candlelight, a quiet sanctuary in the heart of his grand manor. He'd been engrossed in a series of correspondences, managing the myriad affairs of his estate and connections with London society. Despite his playboy reputation, he was a man of significant responsibilities.

As he dipped his quill into the inkwell to pen yet another response, the door to his study swung open with a flourish, heralding the arrival of a force of nature. Lady Beatrice, Alexander's grandmother, made her grand entrance, commanding the room effortlessly. She was a woman of a certain age, yet she carried herself with a regal bearing that could rival any debutante in the ton. Her silver hair was elegantly styled into a chignon, perfectly complementing her attire—an exquisite emerald-green gown that spoke volumes of her enduring fashion sense.

Her piercing blue eyes, sharp as a hawk's, held a mischievous glint, and her lips were curled in an enigmatic smile. Lady Beatrice's allure remained undeniable, a fact that had left many a man bewitched by her charm.

"Alexander, darling." She sauntered further into the room, her voluminous skirts swaying with each step. "I trust I'm not interrupting anything of great importance?"

Alexander's irritation at the interruption melted away instantly. His grandmother had a way of captivating his attention. He regarded her fondly, for in many ways, she had been more of a mother to him than his actual mother had ever been.

"Of course not, Grandmama." He set his quill aside and rose from his chair to greet her with a warm embrace. "Your timing is, as always, impeccable."

Lady Beatrice laughed, a melodious trill. She returned his hug, her presence filling the room with an electric energy. "I couldn't resist the temptation to see my beloved grandson. You've been dreadfully scarce lately."

Alexander leaned back to study her with genuine affection in his heart. "I've been preoccupied with various matters, but I am never too busy for you, Grandmama."

She waved a dismissive hand, her bejeweled fingers sparkling in the candlelight. "Nonsense, my dear boy. We all have our responsibilities. But do indulge an old woman and allow her to share a cup of tea with her favorite grandson."

Alexander smiled and offered his arm to her. "It would be my pleasure."

Together, they made their way to a comfortable seating area, and a servant was promptly summoned to bring tea. As they settled in, Lady Beatrice regaled Alexander with the latest gossip from London society, her stories peppered with witty commentary and keen observations.

Alexander savored these moments with his grandmother. She was a beacon of light in his often complicated life. A source of wisdom, humor, and unconditional love. Her audacity and vivacity had shaped him into the man he was, and he cherished every second they spent together.

As they sipped their tea, ate their finger sandwiches and lost themselves in lively conversation, a profound sense of gratitude for Lady Beatrice's enduring presence in his life filled Alexander. She was the anchor in the tempest of society, the guiding star he could always rely on. And as she held court in his study, he couldn't imagine a more delightful interruption to his daily affairs.

Alexander noticed a mischievous twinkle in her eyes, a sure sign that she was about to propose something audacious. She set her teacup down with a dramatic flourish.

"Alexander, my dear, I've had the most splendid idea," she announced with a gleeful grin.

Alexander raised an eyebrow, fully aware that his grandmother's ideas often led to excitement, scandal, or a combination of both. "Pray, share your splendid idea, Grandmama."

She leaned in closer, her voice dropping to a conspiratorial whisper. "I want to host a ball this very weekend, with no prior notice to the ton. A last-minute affair that will keep them all on their toes."

Alexander couldn't help but chuckle at his grandmother's audacity. A last-minute ball was a feat that very few could pull off successfully, but if anyone could, it was Lady Beatrice.

"Why throw a ball on such short notice?" he inquired with a hint of amusement.

Her eyes sparkled with excitement as she continued, "It will be a grand spectacle, a dazzling display of spontaneity. We shall invite everyone, and the ton will be left in a delightful frenzy, rushing to prepare for an event they had not anticipated."

Alexander was intrigued by the idea. It was just the kind of bold, unconventional plan his grandmother was known for. "A last-minute ball it is, Grandmama. I shall have the invitations sent immediately. It will be a night to remember."

Lady Beatrice clapped her hands with delight, and the two of them began to discuss the logistics of their impromptu gathering. Alexander admired his grandmother's boundless spirit and her penchant for infusing excitement into their lives. As they made their preparations, he was buoyed by the idea that the weekend would bring a great deal of joy and laughter for the Darrow family.

And he'd ensure Eleanor and her sisters came.

He needed to see her again, to persuade her to marry him. And a ball was the perfect time to do it.

Chapter Five

The Darrow kitchen was a hive of activity as the evening meal was prepared. Since they had let most of their staff go, Olivia had taken it upon herself to assist the cook in preparing supper. Eleanor sat at the wooden table half-heartedly going through receipts, but her mind was elsewhere.

Olivia rapped flour-dusted knuckles on the table to get Eleanor's attention.

"Eleanor." Olivia's eyes sparkled with a hint of mischief as Eleanor lifted her gaze briefly. "I don't understand why you will not even consider Lord Weston's proposal. It could be the solution we have been hoping for."

Eleanor sighed as she rubbed at her temples, her gaze fixed on a basket of freshly picked vegetables that lay nearby. She had grappled with the weight of her decision ever since Lord Weston made his offer. He didn't take the rejection well, not that she expected him to.

"I have told you my reasons." Eleanor sighed again. "I do not wish to be beholden to anyone, especially him."

Olivia wiped her hands on her apron, concern etched across her features. "But we are at a crossroads, and Mama's health is deteriorating. We need to consider every option."

Olivia was right, of course, and the burden of responsibility weighed heavily on Eleanor's shoulders. But the thought of accepting Lord Weston's proposal still filled her with cold dread. If only she could discuss this more fully with Olivia. They were close, but Eleanor would not drag her family any further into the mire than necessary.

"I know we do." Eleanor covered Olivia's hand with her own. "But there is more to it than that. Lord Weston and I have a complicated history, one I would rather not revisit."

Olivia nodded in understanding but pressed further. "Sometimes we must make difficult choices for the greater good." She turned back to the food. "Lord Weston's offer could provide stability for Mama and the family, even if it means sacrificing some of our independence."

Except it wouldn't be anyone else's independence that would be lost, it would be hers alone.

Eleanor stood and reached for Olivia's hand, her expression softening. "Please believe me that I will explore other options."

Olivia shook her head. "I must admit, I would be willing to accept Lord Weston's proposal if you are not. He is wealthy, charming, and undeniably handsome."

Eleanor understood the allure of such a match on a logical level. Lord Weston's wealth and good looks were indeed appealing to many. But that wasn't enough. Not for her or her beautiful sister.

Eleanor let out a half laugh, though there was nothing funny at all about this situation. She squeezed Olivia's hand. "Lord Weston would not be faithful. His reputation precedes him, and you couldn't expect otherwise."

Olivia nodded, acknowledging her sister's point. "I suppose you're right. But sometimes, we must make compromises. Fidelity from a husband might be too much to ask for in our circumstances."

Eleanor stilled. It took her a moment to regain her composure. "You can't mean that." They'd grown up surrounded by love. How could Olivia expect anything less?

Olivia, her eyes earnest, met Eleanor's gaze squarely. "I do. I mean it. I have seen how devoted our mother was to Father despite his imperfections. She knew about his mistress, but it did not deter her from loving him."

Eleanor considered her sister's words. Their mother had been a paragon of understanding and forgiveness, but the circumstances were different.

Olivia, however, was adamant. "I am strong enough to love someone like that. I'm not so quick to judge as you."

"Accepting Lord Weston's proposal wouldn't mean a real marriage, and certainly wouldn't mean love. It would be a business transaction. One that would secure our family's future." That was exactly the problem, wasn't it? She'd rejected a proposal that could help unburden her family. Eleanor let out a deep sigh, her heart heavy with the enormity of the decision that lay ahead.

Olivia shook her head, frustration creeping into her voice. "You're treating this like it is personal. If you truly understood our predicament, you would see that Lord Weston is our best option. His wealth and influence could save us. Our family's future is at stake, and we must make pragmatic choices. If you cannot, I will."

Eleanor couldn't deny the validity of Olivia's argument. The weight of their mother's legacy and the family's well-being rested heavily on her, and the choices she would make in the coming days would define their future.

Eleanor considered her sister's perspective. Olivia was right. Sometimes, pragmatism had to take precedence over personal feelings. Family honor and security were paramount, and she would have to find a way to reconcile her principles with the harsh realities of their situation.

As the morning sun streamed through the windows of the sitting room, Caroline burst in with a flourish, a cream-colored envelope in hand. Her cheeks were flushed with excitement, and her eyes sparkled as she waved the correspondence.

"Sisters, look!" Caroline exclaimed, breathless with the news. "An invitation for a ball this evening from Lady Beatrice!"

Olivia and Mary couldn't contain their enthusiasm and joined in with exclamations of delight, their faces lighting up with joy. They gathered around Caroline, their heads no doubt already filled with visions of elegant gowns, sparkling chandeliers, and the thrill of a night out in high society.

Eleanor remained seated, her breath catching in her throat. Should they attend?

Her shoulders tightened with unease regarding the sudden invitation from Lord Weston's grandmother, especially after her recent encounter with the man himself. Her gaze narrowed. Had he talked his grandmother into this sudden event?

Eleanor stood and joined her sisters. "Did this invitation come with a specific purpose or message?"

Caroline frowned, her enthusiasm obviously dampened. "It does not specify. Just that the ball is at Lord Weston's residence tonight, and we are cordially invited."

"We should be grateful for the opportunity," Mary piped up. "A ball at Lord Weston's is not something to be taken lightly."

Eleanor's eyes darted between her excited sisters, her protective instincts kicking in. She couldn't ignore the feeling that Lord Weston had an agenda, especially after his proposal and her rejection. It was as though he were making another move on the intricate chessboard of their lives.

"I do not mean to dampen your spirits." Though, of course, she did. "But we should proceed with care. It is barely six months since our father passed, and Lord Weston is a man of complex intentions. We need to be mindful of the reasons behind this invitation, considering how last minute it is."

"Eleanor is right." Olivia took charge. "We should attend the ball, dressed conservatively, of course, to mark the transition out of mourning, and with our wits about us. We cannot afford to stand out for the wrong reasons or be naive, especially in our current circumstances."

The feeling of unease grew as her sisters scurried to select their dresses. While she understood their excitement and longing to attend a grand social event, the abruptness of the invitation left her with unanswered questions. Her suspicions about Lord Weston's intentions remained, and she couldn't help but wonder why he or his grandmother would throw a ball with such haste.

She sighed. Olivia had postponed her debut season after their father's death, and the chance to finally step back into society was long overdue. No matter her concerns, Eleanor couldn't deny her sister the opportunity to enjoy a proper ball.

Amid the whirlwind of preparations, Eleanor decided to visit Lord Weston before the event and seek answers directly from him. She couldn't attend without knowing the motives behind his sudden invitation. Her duty as the eldest daughter and the guardian of her family's honor compelled her.

Determined and resolute, Eleanor left her sisters to their excitement and hurriedly donned a gown suitable for making afternoon calls. The journey to Lord Weston's residence was a short carriage ride away, but the weight of the unknown pressed heavily on her.

Arriving at Lord Weston's grand manor, Eleanor was escorted inside by the servants and led to the drawing room. She had little time to wait before Lord Alexander Weston himself entered, an air of casual elegance surrounding him, a charming smile on his lips.

"Eleanor. What a pleasant surprise."

Eleanor neither sat nor wasted any time with pleasantries. "Lord Weston, I appreciate the invitation, but I must know the reason behind this last-minute ball. Why have you extended this invitation to my family with such haste?"

Lord Weston's gaze held a hint of intrigue as he regarded her. "I have no hidden agenda here. Grandmother wanted to throw one of her off-the-cuff gatherings, and I simply thought it would be a delightful opportunity for you and your family to enjoy a splendid evening."

Eleanor shook her head. "I need to understand your intentions. Your sudden proposal and now this invitation have left me with more questions than answers."

Lord Weston sighed, his demeanor shifting from casual to more serious. "Very well, Eleanor. I understand your concerns. Let me be candid with you. I am genuinely interested in helping your family. Our previous encounters might have been complicated, but my intentions are sincere. The ball, however, is something my grandmother concocted.

Not I." He lifted a shoulder. "The woman is a force of nature. I cannot refuse my grandmother her whims."

Eleanor considered his words carefully, her suspicions not yet dispelled. The weight of her family's future bore heavily on her shoulders, and she couldn't afford to make any hasty decisions. If they did not accept the invitation and stayed at home, no doubt the gossips would have a field day. If they did all attend as gay as could be, they'd likely be snubbed to their faces.

"I appreciate your candor, Lord Weston." Her tone softened. "But I must remain cautious. My family's security is the upmost importance to me. We will attend the ball, but I will do so with a watchful eye."

He smirked at her in a way that had heat unfurling in her belly. "That is all I can ask."

Chapter Six

Alexander remained in the drawing room after Eleanor's departure, his thoughts tainted with uncertainty. The unexpected visit surprised him, not a position he appreciated. As he contemplated Eleanor and what she could mean for his future, Lady Beatrice entered the room with her customary air of regal authority.

Her piercing blue eyes surveyed him with keen interest. "Alexander, my dear, what was Lady Eleanor doing here? I gather her visit was not a mere social call."

Alexander sighed, running a hand through his tousled hair. "No, Grandmama, it was not. She came to discuss the invitation I sent to her family for the ball."

Lady Beatrice arched a perfectly sculpted brow. "What is your purpose in including them, Alexander? I left them off the list for a reason, knowing what her family has gone through. I hear their mother is still in deep mourning."

Alexander hesitated, struggling to find the right words to explain the situation to his formidable grandmother. "It is a gesture of goodwill. I am genuinely interested in helping the Darrow family, but Eleanor remains cautious and suspicious of my motives."

Lady Beatrice regarded him with a shrewd expression. She'd always had a talent for uncovering the truth.

"Since when are you a man to extend gestures of goodwill without a deeper purpose? What is your true intention regarding the Darrow family?"

Alexander hesitated, knowing that he could not conceal the truth from his grandmother. "I am, in fact, interested in offering Eleanor a partnership, Grandmama. But she remains skeptical, given our complicated history."

Lady Beatrice's eyes glittered with mischief "Partnership, you say? What sort of partnership, my dear?"

Alexander leaned back in his chair, grappling with the weight of the decision he had made. "I want to help the Darrow family regain their standing in society and provide for their future. But Eleanor's doubts and the scandal surrounding her family have made her wary of accepting any assistance."

Lady Beatrice regarded her grandson with a mix of pride and understanding. "Alexander, you have always had a generous heart, and your desire to help the Darrow family is commendable. However, you must tread carefully and be patient with Eleanor. She is a woman of principles and responsibility."

She gave him one of her notorious looks, one with a raised brow and pursed lips.

Alexander appreciated his grandmother's wisdom. "Yes." He huffed. "I'm beginning to understand that."

Lady Beatrice rose from her seat. "Remember that not all battles are won by persuasion alone. Sometimes, it is quiet persistence and genuine intentions that open the door to understanding and trust." She gave him a long look. "You should start getting ready. The ball is only hours away and we want to look our best."

The grand ballroom was a vision of splendor and extravagance. As the evening wore on, the room came to life in a dazzling display of shimmering gowns, glittering jewels, and the lively chatter of high society. The atmosphere was suffused with the sounds of a string quartet, their melodies weaving through the air, enticing couples onto the dance floor.

As the guests twirled and swirled in the waltz, Alexander descended the curved marble steps with an air of quiet authority. He had taken his time preparing for the evening's event, ensuring that his attire was impeccable and befitting his status as the host.

He wore a meticulously tailored black tailcoat, the deep shade accentuating his broad shoulders and commanding presence. A crisp, pristine white shirt and an intricately tied silk cravat adorned his neck, contrasting sharply with the darkness of his attire. His waistcoat, a shade of midnight blue, added a touch of regal elegance to his ensemble, embroidered with silver thread in an intricate pattern that caught the light.

His trousers were of the finest quality, clinging to his legs with a tailored perfection. Highly polished black leather shoes completed the ensemble, reflecting the golden glow of the chandeliers above. Every detail was carefully considered, and his attire conveyed an air of unassuming sophistication, a reflection of his position in society.

As he descended the final steps, the sweeping grandeur of the ballroom unfolded before him. The guests, both familiar faces and new acquaintances, turned to acknowledge his presence with polite nods and smiles. Alexander's gaze swept across the room, noting the array of gowns in hues of emerald, sapphire, and rose, each more resplendent than the last.

The scents of perfumes, the soft rustle of silk, and the gentle murmur of conversation enveloped him as he moved through the ballroom. His presence, always a matter of intrigue, garnered subtle glances and whispers among the attendees.

Alexander was known not only for his wealth and standing but also for his magnetic charm and charismatic personality. It was no surprise that the room came alive as he approached, the guests eager to engage in conversation or share a dance with the enigmatic host.

However, there was one guest whose presence he was particularly interested in. Eleanor Darrow and her family had arrived, and Alexander's gaze sought her out among the attendees. She and her sisters were easy to spot, close together, each of them dark-haired, blue-eyed beauties, so much alike they were never mistaken for anything but sisters. She was an arresting figure in a gown of soft lilac, her dark hair adorned with a simple yet elegant ribbon. Despite her outward grace, there was a sense of guarded reserve in her eyes.

Tonight's ball was not merely a lavish social event, it was a stage upon which their complex dance would continue. Alexander was determined to prove the sincerity of his intentions, to extend a hand of assistance to Eleanor and her family. The evening would bring challenges and revelations, and he was prepared to face them.

As he made his way through the ballroom, Alexander's gaze remained fixed on Eleanor. It was then he realized she was speaking with Lord Satterfield. A flicker of possessiveness sparked within him. He had always been protective of her, and the sight of her with another man set his teeth on edge.

As the music swirled around them, Alexander approached the couple. "Lord Satterfield," he said, his tone polite. Then he turned to Eleanor. "Might I have this dance, Lady Eleanor?"

Lord Satterfield, obviously not wanting to cause any discord, graciously excused himself. "Of course, Lord Weston," he said, bowing his head. "Lady Eleanor, it has been a pleasure."

Eleanor stiffened but did not refuse his request. She met his eyes with a cautious expression and offered a slight nod. "Of course, Lord Weston."

As the waltz reached its crescendo, Alexander extended his hand, and Eleanor placed her gloved fingers into his. They stepped onto the dance floor, their movements in perfect harmony with the music. The physical closeness, the graceful turns and twirls, brought back a rush of memories, both tender and tumultuous.

"May I say, Lady Eleanor, you look beautiful this evening," Alexander remarked, his voice low and filled with genuine admiration.

Eleanor offered a small smile in response. "Thank you, Lord Weston. The same could be said for your impeccable taste in hosting such a magnificent ball."

They glided through the dance, but Alexander could sense Eleanor's reluctance, and he didn't blame her. After all, only a few days ago she'd rejected his marriage proposal. That would be enough to set anyone on edge.

He was not one to shy away from a challenge though. This dance was not just a dance, it was a symbol of his intent to bridge the gap that had divided them for so long.

As the music from their waltz slowly faded into the background, Alexander let curiosity get the better of him. He cast a polite smile in Eleanor's direction and kept his tone casual. "Do you know Lord Satterfield well?"

Eleanor regarded Alexander with a hint of annoyance. "Lord Satterfield is a respectable gentleman. You know quite well that he comes from a well-regarded family, and his manners are impeccable. I find his company quite pleasant."

Alexander raised an eyebrow, a faint trace of skepticism in his expression. "Impeccable manners, you say?" He cocked his head to the side. "Well, that may be true, but I find he lacks the certain spark that distinguishes a true gentleman."

Eleanor chuckled softly at Alexander's critique. "I believe you are being quite critical. Not every man is expected to possess the same qualities, and Lord Satterfield has his own charm."

Alexander's gaze remained fixed on her, his tone earnest. "My dear Eleanor, you deserve nothing but the best. Lord Satterfield, for all his respectability, may not be the best match for someone as exceptional as you. For one, he's old. He already has grown children. He—"

"I have no interest in wedding Lord Satterfield, if that is what you think." Eleanor interrupted him. "Not that's any of your business. I am quite capable of making my own judgments."

"I do not doubt your judgment, my lady." Alexander's lips curved into a wry grin. "But I have a vested interest in your happiness and well-being."

"That is not my concern." Her eyes narrowed.

"It should be," he insisted. "Time is of the essence, and—"

"I shall be the one to worry about time." Her tone was becoming increasingly sharp.

"He will not be able to help you. Not like I can."

Their exchange had taken on an edge, and Alexander was acutely aware of the eyes that lingered on them. Their situation could not be discussed openly on the crowded dance floor, and he sought a more private setting to address the pressing matters at hand.

"Eleanor." He locked his gaze with hers. "Allow me to walk with you in the gardens. We can continue our conversation in private, away from prying ears."

She stared at him for a long moment before finally agreeing. "Very well." She gave a single nod. "But we must have a chaperone. I will not compromise my reputation."

Alexander nodded in agreement, relieved that she had accepted his suggestion. "Of course. We shall find a suitable chaperone and proceed discreetly."

Milly, one of the older maids, a female of suitable age and character, was more than willing to accompany them to the garden. With a graceful curtsey, she offered to escort them and ensure the propriety of their meeting.

As they stepped out into the moonlit gardens, the cool night air provided a welcome respite from the heated atmosphere of the ballroom. The chaperone, giving them a polite distance, allowed Alexander and Eleanor to walk side by side along the meandering paths illuminated by the soft glow of lanterns.

The shadows cast by the garden's flora danced around them, and the gentle rustling of leaves provided a soothing backdrop to their conversation. The night held an air of serenity that was a stark contrast to the intensity of their previous exchange.

"Eleanor, I understand your reservations and the weight of responsibility that rests upon your shoulders," Lord Weston said. "But I am determined to assist you and your family in any way I can. You do not have to face this challenge alone."

Eleanor regarded him with a keen gaze. "I appreciate your willingness to help, Lord Weston, but I must ensure that any partnership we enter is for the benefit of my family and not merely out of necessity. I will not compromise. I do not understand why I must repeat myself."

"Because you are being stubborn." he said. "You reject me only because of our history—"

"That is enough of a reason."

"And you will not allow me the benefit of the doubt," he said. "I have changed. The man you knew then—"

"Men do not change." Eleanor jolted to a stop. "I cannot risk—"

She didn't understand how much he wanted her, that was obvious. She thought he was doing this out of charity. He couldn't have that. So, before she could finish that sentence, he reached out and grabbed her by the waist.

Her eyes went wide, and her lips parted perfectly for his kiss.

Chapter Seven

Alexander's kiss wasn't rough or awkward. It was perfection. His lips brushed against hers with a feather-light touch that had her leaning towards him, needing more. Only then did he deepen the kiss, making her whole body sing. The kiss was a revelation, a heady combination of tenderness and intensity.

Eleanor's initial hesitation gave way to a surge of emotions, and she responded with a passion that had long been suppressed. The kiss was a bittersweet blend of longing and connection, a testament to the undeniable chemistry that had always existed between them.

The garden witnessed their unspoken words, their desires laid bare in the moonlit shadows. For a stolen moment, the complexities of their lives and the weight of their responsibilities faded into the background, leaving only the intoxicating sensation of their kiss.

As the kiss gradually slowed, they remained locked in a lingering embrace, their foreheads touching as they caught their breath. Eleanor's heart raced, her mind a whirlwind of conflicting emotions. She had allowed herself to be swept away by the fervor of the moment, but the challenges of their intricate dance still loomed on the horizon.

Eleanor's voice trembled. She was breathless. She stepped away, needing space. "Why did you do that?"

Alexander's gaze bored into hers. "I had to. I have been wanting to kiss you for a long time now."

She couldn't deny the powerful connection they'd shared in that stolen moment. But fear gnawed at the edges of her heart. "But someone could have seen! I would have been ruined, my reputation tarnished. We would have been forced to marry." Her eyes narrowed. Suddenly, it made sense. The last-minute ball, the dance, the walk where they would be alone, save for an old woman who worked for him. "You did this on purpose."

Alexander's gaze widened, and he shook his head earnestly. "You think I planned to ruin you? Don't be ridiculous."

Despite his protests, Eleanor couldn't shake the feeling that their kiss had not been a mere act of spontaneity.

"Ridiculous?" Her voice laced was with frustration. "You are cunning and manipulative, Alexander Weston. You always get your way, no matter what. Always. And you want me to think your passion for me overcame your sensibilities?"

Alexander took a step closer, his voice unwavering. "What must I do to prove myself to you? To prove I only want to help?"

The intensity of their exchange hung like heavy smog in the air. But Eleanor's guarded heart remained a formidable barrier, and she was acutely aware of the challenges that lay ahead.

The bushes beside them rustled. Footsteps on the path tiptoed away.

Someone had been there.

Someone had seen *them.*

An uneasy shiver raced down her spine. Her worst fears might be coming true. Heart pounding in her chest, she held her breath, waiting for the death knock. Her gaze darted towards the source of the disturbance.

Alexander took a step closer. "I will protect you." He held his hand over his heart as if making a solemn vow. "I will marry you and ensure your family's well-being."

Eleanor's gaze pierced his, and she found herself at a crossroads. Her heart was torn between the past and the future, between the familiar and the unknown. "I would rather marry Lord Satterfield than marry you. I cannot trust you. I do not think I'll ever be able to trust you."

The shock and anger that flared in Alexander's eyes were impossible to miss. He grabbed Eleanor, pushing her against the wall. His voice was a low, vehement growl. "There is no way in hell I would let you marry Satterfield."

Eleanor, her frustration and anger matching his intensity, pushed back against his words. "You do not have the privilege of telling me what to do."

Alexander's eyes locked onto hers as he posed a question that cut to the heart of their complex relationship. "If I did, would you even listen?"

The tension between them crackled in the air, and the moonlit garden seemed to hold its breath. Their intricate dance had reached a critical juncture, and the choices they made in this moment would shape their future in ways they couldn't yet fathom.

"Would you be a good girl and obey?" he asked, leaning closer to her.

Eleanor's core pulsed with want. She hated how he made her feel, how his mere presence could ignite a fire in her loins. But she loved it too. Loved the rush of desire that consumed her whenever they were together. No doubt, he felt the same way. It was the reason they argued with such ferocity, and why they couldn't seem to stay away from each other.

She tried to push away the desire to give in to his command, but the way he looked at her made it difficult to refuse. The intensity in his eyes reminded her of what drew her to him. He was a force to be reckoned with, and she was powerless against him.

But she couldn't let him win, not this time. She needed to stand her ground and make him see she was no longer willing to be his puppet.

"I do not need your permission to make my own choices, Alexander." Eleanor stiffened her spine. "I can make my own decisions, and I choose Lord Satterfield. He is a kind and honorable man, and he will make me happy."

Alexander's eyes darkened with a mix of frustration and desire. "I could make you happy too, Eleanor. In ways that Lord Satterfield could never even imagine."

Eleanor's heart raced as Alexander's breath brushed her neck. He could give her pleasure no other man could match, but she couldn't let him control her life.

"I must go." She tried to push him away. As much as Eleanor craved intoxication within his embrace, the weight of her responsibilities laid heavy on her. She couldn't afford to let him control her life, to jeopardize her family's honor. The echoes of their tumultuous history reverberated in her mind, a reminder of the dangers of their illicit connection.

"I have to go." Her voice trembled with both desire and regret.

Alexander's fingers tightened on her waist, his gaze imploring her to stay. He longed to pull her closer, to taste the forbidden sweetness of their passion once more. The mounting tension between them was palpable, the unspoken yearning in their eyes a testament to their shared torment.

A pang of frustration and longing coursed through him as he reluctantly released her. He understood the duty and honor that bound her, but his own desires were no less powerful. "Eleanor," he murmured, his voice thick with longing, "Please stay."

Eleanor, torn between her heart's desire and her sense of responsibility, took a step back, the distance between them growing with each passing moment. She hated she'd pulled away from him, despised the barriers that stood between them, but the stakes were too high. The complexities of their past and the uncertainties of their future demanded restraint, even as her heart ached for the embrace she couldn't allow herself to indulge in.

As she turned to leave, the mounting tension between them remained, a lingering ache that mirrored the bittersweet undercurrent of their intricate dance. Their paths had diverged, duty and honor leading the way, even as their hearts yearned for the forbidden passion they could no longer share.

"You will regret this," he called after her.

Under her breath, she murmured, "I already do."

Eleanor stepped away from the moonlit garden, her heart heavy with the weight of unfulfilled desire. She was intercepted by her three sisters on the terrace and everything else faded away. Their keen eyes detected the turmoil in her expression and traces of unshed tears in her eyes.

Olivia was the first to speak. "Eleanor, what happened? You look so distraught."

Caroline and Mary exchanged worried glances, sensing that something had gone awry during Eleanor's encounter in the garden.

"No," she said. "Of course not."

She tried to wipe moisture from her eyes without being obvious, but a tear rolled down her cheek. "Are you enjoying yourselves?"

Olivia rolled her eyes. "We are ready to leave."

Mary nodded in agreement, her inexperienced eyes filled with concern. "It is rather boring, and if I am to be bored, I would rather be bored at home."

"Well, if you're sure." Eleanor gulped.

"We are," Caroline said, though Eleanor could detect something else in her tone, something akin to longing. Then again, she could be hearing things.

"Gather your things." Olivia scrubbed her wet cheeks dry. "We should slip away before anyone notices—"

Before Olivia could finish her sentence, Alexander's grandmother joined them on the terrace. Her piercing gaze held Eleanor's. "Lady Eleanor. "I hope you are not leaving. You and I have much to discuss."

Chapter Eight

Eleanor was led through the grand halls of Lord Alexander Weston's imposing estate by none other than Alexander's spirited and saucy grandmother, Lady Beatrice Constance Weston. The older woman had always held a particular fondness for her, often referring to her as the granddaughter she never had.

"Come along, my dear." Lady Beatrice stepped briskly as she guided Eleanor towards the study. "There is something we must discuss away from prying ears, and we must act now."

Eleanor's curiosity piqued, and she followed without protest, wondering what might be of such importance that her presence was required in Lord Weston's study. As they reached the door, Lady Beatrice pushed it open and gestured for her to enter.

Eleanor stepped inside. Alexander stood by the window, his hands clasped behind his back. His expression was inscrutable, a mix of concern and determination. The flickering candlelight cast deep shadows across his face, emphasizing the intensity in his eyes.

"Alexander." Eleanor halted. "What is the meaning of this?"

Lady Beatrice, her eyes twinkling with mischief, closed the door behind her with a knowing smile.

Alexander took a step closer, his gaze unwavering as he broke the silence. "Grandmother? What is going on here?"

Eleanor couldn't help the feeling of unease. She watched him like a hawk, searching for clues in his expression, but he seemed just as confused as she was.

"Forgive the interruption, my dears," Lady Beatrice said, "but I believe there are matters of urgency we must address."

"Multiple people have approached me," Lady Beatrice continued, "and they have mentioned seeing the two of you in the garden together. The ton is abuzz with whispers, and your family's honor is at stake, Eleanor."

Eleanor's eyes widened, and her heart sank as she realized the gravity of the situation. The consequences of their encounter in the garden could have far-reaching implications for her family.

Her gaze hardened as the weight of their predicament settled upon her. Suspicious, her emotions stirred by the potential consequences of their encounter, her voice trembled with accusation as she turned her gaze to Alexander. "You did this on purpose, didn't you?"

Alexander's expression was a mix of incredulity and protest. "Eleanor, I would do nothing to ruin you. You must believe me."

But Eleanor was unrelenting, and her voice remained resolute. "Even if it that ruination keeps me away from Lord Satterfield?"

Lady Beatrice, who had been listening attentively, interjected with a hint of her characteristic candor, "Certainly, you do not need to ruin yourself to keep yourself away from that old man."

Alexander's grandmother, with her usual forthrightness, took a deep breath and addressed the issue at hand. "As of right now, it is nothing more than a rumor. But considering your history, and that you left together to walk the garden..." Her voice trailed off, leaving the implication hanging in the air.

Eleanor's heart sank as the gravity of the situation became apparent. The whispers and speculations of the ton had the potential to cast a shadow over her family. No one knew better than she the delicate balance they had to maintain to protect their honor. Their past had woven a complicated narrative. The intricacies of their relationship, their shared history, and the unspoken desires between them were all factors that played into the rumors.

A tense moment of time dragged on until Eleanor couldn't stand another moment. "What do we do?"

"We have several options, my dear," Beatrice began. "First, we can attempt to suppress the rumors. Engaging in discreet conversations with those who have heard the whispers and assuring them of your innocence may help contain the situation."

Eleanor nodded, absorbing the older woman's advice. The ton's gossip could be both a blessing and a curse, and countering it with the truth was a wise approach.

Beatrice continued, "Second, you publicly distance yourself from Alex. Attend social events separately or express your disinterest in any engagement with him in a manner that does not overtly draw attention."

Eleanor weighed this option, and considering their interconnecting social circles, it would severely constrain her social life. Worth it, if making herself a social outcast quelled the rumors.

Lady Beatrice broke the silence that had fallen upon the room. "If the situation escalates beyond our control, you will be left with a betrothal, one that safeguards your reputation and aligns with your family's best interests."

The prospect of an engagement with Lord Alexander Weston hung unspoken in the air. Eleanor's heart fluttered at the thought, but it was a decision that could not be taken lightly.

Beatrice leaned forward in her chair, her expression growing increasingly serious. "Hear me out, my dear. Time is of the essence. Rumors in the ton have a way of spreading like wildfire, and we have only a limited window in which to control the narrative. What we decide in the next few days will determine the course of both our families' future. You must act swiftly, Eleanor, and with careful consideration."

Eleanor nodded. She had always been the responsible and dutiful one in her family, shouldering the burden of maintaining their status in society after her father's passing. Now, faced with the potential scandal and rumors that threatened their name, she found herself at a loss.

Beatrice regarded her with a mixture of affection and concern. "You have a strength within, my dear, and a resilience that I have always admired. You must draw upon that now."

Eleanor took a deep breath, steeling herself for the challenges ahead. The intricate dance of society, the expectations, and the complexities of her relationship with Alexander were all factors that added layers of difficulty to the situation.

"What is your counsel?" Eleanor asked.

Beatrice offered a gentle, reassuring smile. "My counsel is to consider the options but don't forget, the choices you make are not just for your sake but also for the future of your sisters and your mother as well."

Eleanor, her mind entangled in a web of uncertainty, turned to Alexander. She couldn't believe she was asking for his opinion, especially since she wouldn't be surprised if he had orchestrated this to happen in the first place, but she needed guidance, and she trusted he would know what to do.

"What do you believe we should do?" she asked quietly.

Alexander's eyes widened, just as surprised by her question as she was. Regardless, he met her gaze with an unwavering determination. "Eleanor, I am prepared to do whatever you desire. I will support you, protect your family's honor, and ensure your happiness, whatever that looks like for you."

His response took Eleanor by surprise, and she was overwhelmed by a sense of relief and gratitude. She thought he'd insist on marriage.

No.

She didn't want to notice his kindness. It could very well be a trap, and she refused to fall into it again.

However, she couldn't deny that she appreciated this from him.

Eleanor's voice quivered with emotion. "Your support means more to me than words can convey, Alexander. I am grateful for your willingness to assist me."

Beatrice, who had been silently observing the exchange, nodded in approval. "I understand you might be hesitant to trust Alexander and myself in this, but I can assure you, we both want what is best for you and your sisters."

The not so subtle reminder of the risk to her sisters' marriage prospects turned Eleanor's thoughts into a swirling whirlpool of uncertainty. The intricacies of the situation bore down on her, and she grappled with the weight of the choices that lay ahead.

No matter how hard they tried, could they even suppress the rumors? Would engaging in discreet conversations with those who had heard the whispers contain the situation, or would the denials spread the gossip even further?

Distancing herself from Alexander couldn't work. Besides doing nothing to quell the rumors, it would still leave her as a social outcast and their family's name dragged through mud.

The prospect of an engagement with Alex was tantalizing, yet it also carried the baggage of their shared history and uncertain future.

Her sense of duty to her family and the desire to safeguard their reputation waged a silent war against her personal desires.

"I would make you an honorable husband." Alexander took her hand in his.

She lifted her eyes to meet his, and her breath caught in her throat. There was an intensity there she didn't expect, like he needed her to believe him. He needed her to know that he was telling her the truth.

His grandmother faded away until it was just the two of them, locked in a stare from which Eleanor couldn't free herself.

"I–" She swallowed. What could she say to that?

She didn't know.

Biting her bottom lip, she ignored the way her cheeks pinched with a blush. She didn't want to trust him.

He had already proved his infidelity and broken her heart. She was sure, if given the chance, he'd do it again, and she'd be an even bigger fool than before.

But she wanted to believe him, and that scared her more than anything.

Before she could respond, the door burst open and Olivia, Mary, and Caroline stumbled in.

"Eleanor." Olivia was breathless. "We heard...what they're saying... they are saying awful, awful things."

"What?" Beatrice stood slowly. "What, exactly, are people saying?"

Olivia looked between Eleanor and Alexander, her face bright red.

Eleanor pressed her lips into a thin line. Without speaking, Olivia had said everything that needed to be said.

Chapter Nine

A heavy sense of guilt settled in the pit of Alexander's stomach. The damage was done. Nothing he could do now would put things right.

Eleanor stood stock still, her eyes wide, her whole body quaking. It took every ounce of self-control not to scoop her into his arms.

Damn it. Rumors would be flying from one end of the ballroom to the other. Eleanor and her family name may never recover from this. Their position had not been solid before tonight, and now the shadows were even deeper, the journey back into society's graces even harder. His own actions, those moments in the garden and the whispers of their history, had played a part in the suffering Eleanor now endured.

A profound sense of responsibility weighed on Alexander's conscience. He had always considered himself a protector of Eleanor, someone who would shield her from harm. Yet in this instance, he was the catalyst for the rumors that threatened her honor.

It was too late now to misdirect the rumor mill, and no amount of Eleanor distancing herself from him would mend her reputation. They were well and truly ensnared.

He wanted to reassure Eleanor, to promise her that he would stand by her side no matter what. But he couldn't erase the guilt that gnawed at him. He had not only failed to protect her from the whispers and the judgment of the ton, he'd made her situation so much worse.

He had to set things right. At that moment, he silently vowed to stand by Eleanor, not only as a protector but as a partner. The damage had been done, but together, they would find a way to reclaim their families' honor and rewrite the narrative that threatened to define them.

Eleanor stroked her throat as if needing help to swallow, her voice, resolute and unwavering. "We must marry."

Alexander's brain stopped working. A sense of paralysis overtook him. Of all the things he'd expected Eleanor to say, that was not it. He wrangled his thoughts into order and opened his mouth to respond, to offer reassurance and understanding, but she cut him off before he could utter a word.

"You must know how difficult this is for me." Eleanor's chin quivered. "But I will do what I must to save my family's reputation."

Nothing about her own reputation, of course. She was thinking of her sisters and their marriage prospects. Her internal struggle was clear in her eyes, but the weight of responsibility she carried on her shoulders did not weigh her down. He admired her strength, selflessness and her unwavering commitment to her family's honor.

Lady Beatrice took charge before Alexander moved. "Welcome to the family, my dear. I will take care of everything."

Alexander raised an eyebrow and turned to his grandmother. "What are you planning, Grandmama?"

Lady Beatrice gave a slight shrug. "I will instruct the servants to discreetly spread rumors that Lady Eleanor and Lord Weston have been secretly engaged for some time, and that he was merely overwhelmed with passion for her."

The sisters exchanged puzzled glances. No doubt, Olivia, Caroline, and Mary were aware of his proposal and Eleanor's rejection and were uncertain about the sudden change in direction. Lady Beatrice's unexpected strategy had taken them by surprise.

Lady Beatrice's eyes sparkled with mischief. She was never happier than when she was in the thick of things. "My dear, sometimes the best way to quell one rumor is to create another."

"Wait." Olivia held up her hands, her nose wrinkling. "But what is happening, Eleanor? Why have you suddenly changed your mind? Why not just deny the rumors?"

Eleanor rubbed at her arms as if she were cold despite the warmth in the small room.

Beatrice took charge again. "These are not the sort of rumors that can simply be denied. Not if we want to ensure Eleanor's reputation is intact."

Mary clapped her hands together in delight. "Well, I think it's wonderful! I cannot wait to be a bridesmaid."

Caroline jammed her arms across her chest. "But you were so adamant, Eleanor."

Alexander stepped in. "I am marrying Eleanor because I love her, and I want what is best for her and her family." He spoke with the kind of authority that suggested no further discussion was required.

Eleanor's sisters exchanged glances, their expressions now a mix of relief and understanding. Alexander's declaration seemed to clear the air and put their minds at ease.

He hoped it had, at least.

Mary beamed with joy. "It is like a fairy tale, Eleanor. You will have your happily ever after."

Olivia remained silent. Her gaze darted between Eleanor and Alexander, and it was clear that she was processing the situation in her own way.

"I do not understand why the two of you split up in the first place," Mary said. "You were always so happy with him, Eleanor—"

"*Mary,*" Eleanor hushed her in a whisper.

As the conversation swirled around them, Alexander's gaze remained fixed on Eleanor. He couldn't help but wish that their situation hadn't unfolded under the shadow of a scandal. He wished he could have pursued her in a more conventional, romantic way. But despite the unconventional circumstances, he found himself incapable of regretting the decision to marry her.

In that moment, his heart swelled with affection for Eleanor, and regret at what he had lost. She was a strong, intelligent, and principled woman, and he had admired her from the very beginning. Their shared history, with all its challenges, had only deepened his feelings for her.

Their journey together would be filled with hurdles, but he was prepared to face them, hand in hand with her.

"Now that I have agreed to marry, we must plan the wedding carefully." Eleanor began to pace back and forth across the room, her eyes on the floor. Her shoulders were rolled back, resolute, but there was a tremble to her lips, one probably only he noticed. "It should be a celebration that solidifies our union, as if this is always what was meant to be."

Alexander nodded in agreement, his gaze on her unwavering. "The wedding must be grand and memorable, a spectacle that will captivate society's attention and overshadow any lingering doubts."

"I think it should be a magical affair, something that people will talk about for years to come," Mary added in a whimsical voice.

"While the wedding should be grand, it must also be perfect." Caroline raised her hand. "We don't want any more scandals or sensationalism."

Olivia, who had remained somewhat reserved throughout the discussion, finally spoke up. "What about the timing?" she asked. Alexander didn't think she had completely come around to him by any means, but the fact that she was joining the conversation was enough for now. "How soon can we have the wedding?"

Eleanor exchanged a glance with Alexander, a silent acknowledgment of the complexities of their situation. "We mustn't rush into it, but we also shouldn't wait too long. A carefully planned ceremony in a few months should give us the time we need to ensure that all preparations are in place."

"A few months?" Beatrice asked. "It needs to be sooner rather than later, my dear. We are, after all, pretending that you two have been secretly engaged for some time. It would certainly make sense that you would delay an engagement announcement until the mourning time passed."

"How soon?" Eleanor asked, her voice flat.

"This weekend," Beatrice replied.

Mary squealed and clapped. Caroline's eyes widened. Olivia gasped. Eleanor turned quite pale. "This coming weekend?"

"The sooner you wed, the sooner everyone will stop talking about the garden affair and move onto something else." Lady Beatrice waved a dismissive hand. "Not to worry. I shall take care of the details, unless you wish to contribute. I understand many young girls dream of their wedding day, and since this is to be your *only* wedding, I would never want to take that from you."

"That is fine," Eleanor said, her voice tight. "In fact, I would prefer not to think about it."

"If you're sure?"

"I am." Eleanor forced a smile.

Alexander looked away. He couldn't escape the weight of the guilt that settled upon him as he observed Eleanor's demeanor. He had always imagined his bride filled with excitement and giddy joy, but their circumstances were far from conventional. The knowledge that she was being forced into this marriage, not out of love but out of necessity, weighed heavily on his conscience. But he would make up for this uncertain beginning and bring Eleanor happiness.

He cleared his throat, needing to say something. The heavy silence was too much for him. "The guest list is crucial. We must invite influential figures and the ton elite to solidify our place in society."

Eleanor looked at him a long moment. Something flickered in her eyes, and he hated that he didn't know what that was. He used to know her so well.

"I am not sure if Mother..." Eleanor's words trailed off.

Lady Beatrice gently laid her hand on Eleanor's arm. "I will meet with you and your mother tomorrow. I know it is usual for the bride's mother to organize her wedding, but I will make sure she is as involved as much or as little as she is comfortable with."

Eleanor turned to Alexander. "Then I believe it is time for us to head home. I must inform my mother and the staff. There's much to be done, and we must ensure everything is in order."

"I shall walk you out." Alexander rose.

Beatrice nodded. "This is when you must present yourselves as an engaged couple, heads held high, the picture of young love."

Alexander sucked in a breath, hoping no one noticed. Instead, he offered his arm to Eleanor. She stared at it, probably wishing she could do anything else, and the thought gutted him because he deserved her disdain.

Finally, she took it.

Her nearness was a bewitchment, her warmth intoxicating. Her grip was light, and he wished she would clutch him tighter. Instead, he led her out of his study and back into the throng of guests.

As they made their exit from the gathering, curious glances and whispered conversations followed them. At first, he assumed they were directed at them, a couple touched by scandal. However, the more he observed, the clearer it became that the guests' intense scrutiny was focused on Eleanor. The whispers, the sneers, the clouds of judgment, all at her and not him.

He clenched his fingers into tight fists before releasing them.

They walked together toward the door, and, in the public eye, Eleanor complied with the decorum. But when they reached her waiting carriage, she tugged her arm from his.

"I promise, Eleanor," he whispered so no one could overhear. "I'll make this right."

She glared at him, open and defiant. "I think you've done enough."

Ushering her sisters into their shabby carriage, Eleanor didn't look at him once. And he didn't expect her to. When the door snapped shut, he was broken from her spell. Even so, he couldn't find it in him to move.

Not yet.

Alexander stood in the dimly lit courtyard, his gaze fixed on the departing carriage that carried Eleanor and her sisters away. The soft clatter of hooves and the creaking of wheels echoed through the night as the vehicle faded from view. His heart ached with a mixture of emotions, from the weight of responsibility to the longing that stirred within him. He watched until the carriage disappeared around a corner, fading into the obscurity of the city.

He would make their union a source of strength and security for Eleanor and her family, no matter the challenges that lay ahead.

Chapter Ten

The grand chandeliers in the mansion's hallway cast a warm and soft light as Lady Eleanor guided her younger sisters toward their chambers. The evening's events had been overwhelming, and Eleanor longed for the quiet of her own thoughts, even if just for a moment.

As they ascended the ornate staircase, Mary's youthful curiosity bubbled to the surface. "Eleanor, did Lord Alexander really propose to you?"

Caroline chimed in, "You will marry him, won't you?"

"Leave her alone!" Olivia snapped, arms crossed tightly over her chest.

Eleanor shot Olivia a look before managing a tired smile. "Yes, Lord Alexander did propose, and yes, we are going to marry. But it is late now, and we can discuss it more in the morning."

The sisters exchanged knowing glances. Their inquisitive natures were not easily quelled, but thankfully, this time they respected Eleanor's weariness and kept their questions to themselves.

She helped Mary prepare for bed, tucking her in and ensuring she was comfortable. Mary, her big, innocent eyes still filled with wonder, couldn't resist one more question. "Eleanor, do you love him?"

Eleanor chuckled softly and kissed her younger sister's forehead. She wasn't sure how to answer. If she spoke the truth, it might shatter Mary's dream of marrying for love.

Her heart thudded. Maybe it was true. Maybe everything she buried deep inside of her was starting to come back. "I feel a lot of things for Lord Weston." She pinched Mary's cheek. "Bed now."

With a satisfied smile, the girl closed her eyes.

Eleanor checked on Caroline, who had already begun to undress. "What will you wear, Ellie?"

Eleanor shook her head. "No idea. But that is why I have you, right? You will help me find the most suitable dress for the occasion."

"Big and white, layered, with pearls and lace and—"

"We will have to select from my wardrobe." Eleanor patted Caroline on the head. "We can discuss your suggestions in the morning."

When she stepped out of the room, Olivia was waiting for her, arms still crossed over her chest.

"Not you too," Eleanor said as she made her way down the hall.

"Are you sure about this?" Olivia followed her hurried footsteps.

Eleanor paused, her gaze distant for a moment. Love was a complex and multifaceted emotion, and she had many reasons for agreeing to the engagement. However, she wasn't in the mood to delve into such profound matters tonight.

"Liv, this isn't something I'm ready to discuss. Please."

Olivia gave her a long stare, stopping just outside her bedroom door. "You don't have to do this, you know," she said. "We'll survive. We'll figure out—"

"I do," Eleanor said. She rolled her shoulders back, taking a steady breath. "I made a mistake, and now I must take responsibility for it before it casts its net and ensnares all of you."

"But, Eleanor—"

"I will hear no more of this." Her voice was firm, brokering no room for argument. "Olivia, please. I have had a long day and an even longer night. I want to sleep. We can discuss things in the morning."

Olivia looked like she wanted to argue. In fact, she opened her mouth...but shut it. Eleanor's shoulders sagged in relief. Olivia gave one quick, resolute nod before disappearing to her room and softly shutting the door.

Eleanor entered her room, the weight of the day almost smothering her.

The previous twelve hours had been filled with unexpected twists and turns, and the sudden engagement had left her with a swirl of emotions not yet fully processed.

Though her sisters' inquiries were well-intentioned, Eleanor needed time to gather her thoughts, to understand her own feelings, and to prepare herself for the coming days.

She moved to her vanity, the soft candlelight casting a warm and gentle glow across the room. Her fingers deftly undid the intricate buttons of her ball gown, allowing the fabric to fall in graceful folds around her.

With a quiet sigh, she reached for the delicate nightgown laid out on the plush seat beside her. Its soft silk fabric shimmered in the candlelight, perhaps symbolizing the new path she was embarking on—a path that had taken an unexpected turn first with Lord Alexander's proposal, and now with her forthcoming marriage to him.

As she slipped into the garment, Eleanor's thoughts meandered through the labyrinth of emotions that had accompanied the engagement. She couldn't help but think of the strong, determined woman who had come before her, and how she had navigated the intricacies of high society.

She was following in her mother's footsteps, taking on the responsibility of securing her family's future. The weight of that responsibility pressed on her shoulders, and she couldn't deny the unease that came with it. Her mother had been a source of strength and resilience. Did she possess the same qualities?

Her reflection caught her by surprise. The woman staring back at her looked resigned to her future.

Her fiancé was a man of charm, wealth, and enigmatic charisma. Though their engagement was not a result of love, she couldn't deny the admiration she held for his willingness to step forward and offer his support. She respected the sense of honor and duty he brought to their arrangement.

But as she looked at her reflection, Eleanor couldn't help but wonder what the future held for her. Mother would advise her to embrace the journey, to face it with courage and resilience. Eleanor took a deep breath and allowed a sense of determination to settle within her.

Her mother.

Before she could stop herself, she moved to the door.

The corridors of the family estate were shrouded in darkness as Eleanor moved silently, guided only by the soft moonlight that filtered through the windows. Her destination was her mother's room, a space that held both cherished memories and a deep sense of loss.

As she gently pushed open the door, the room was bathed in a silvery glow, revealing the graceful and feminine decor that was her mother's personal touch. The canopy bed was an elegant sanctuary, its curtains now drawn back to reveal the peaceful figure resting within. Eleanor's mother lay in tranquil slumber, her chest rising and falling in a rhythm that mirrored the comforting lull of the night.

She would have taken laudanum to send her to sleep like she did every evening since their father passed. A profound longing for the guidance and comfort her mother had always provided filled Eleanor.

She approached the bedside, her mother's face illuminated by the pale moonlight. Eleanor's brow creased with the weight of her own concerns.

A soft breeze rustled the curtains. Eleanor reached out and brushed her fingers against her mother's cheek, a tender caress for the woman who had taught her the strength and grace she carried with her into every aspect of her life.

In the dimly lit room, Lady Eleanor's emotions overwhelmed her as she knelt by her mother's bedside. Her quiet sobs broke the stillness of the night, and her tear-filled eyes gazed upon her mother's peaceful face. Now that she was alone, she could finally allow herself to feel, to emote, no longer needing to be strong.

"Mother." Eleanor's voice quivered with vulnerability. "I need your help. I don't know if I've done the right thing, and I'm so afraid of the consequences. Please, show me the way."

Her pleas fell upon the slumbering ears of her mother, who remained in peaceful repose, offering no answers or comfort. The room was silent, save for the sound of Eleanor's desperate sobs.

Eleanor would have to navigate this intricate path on her own, making choices and facing consequences with a strength and determination that was uniquely hers.

With a deep breath, Eleanor wiped away her tears and rose from her knees. Her mother's spirit and the lessons she had imparted would always be with her, guiding her in ways that transcended the confines of the physical world.

As she left the room, Eleanor carried with her not only the weight of her mother's legacy but also a newfound resolve. She would face the challenges and uncertainties that lay ahead, relying on her own strength, her love for her family, and the grace her mother had instilled in her.

The quiet of the night surrounded her, and as she walked back to her own room, she was determined to find her own path, just as her mother had before her.

Chapter Eleven

The following day, Eleanor awoke with a sense of renewed purpose. Sunlight streamed through the windows of the family estate, casting a warm and inviting glow across every room, but anticipation and trepidation warred in her as she descended the grand staircase.

She entered the family's drawing room and jolted still. Overnight, it had transformed into a bustling hive of activity. Mary, Olivia, and Caroline chattered excitedly about the goings-on in the household. The room was adorned with fresh flowers that had seemingly sprung to life miraculously, their vibrant colors and fragrant scents filling the air. It was as if the manor had awakened from a long slumber, ready to embrace a new chapter in the family's history.

Mary seemed enthralled by the floral arrangements. Her wide, innocent eyes sparkled with delight as she twirled amidst the blossoms, her fingers brushing against the delicate petals. "Eleanor, look at this! It's like a garden in here."

Olivia and Caroline, both of whom had always been more reserved, shared knowing glances and whispered among themselves. It was clear they were caught up in the excitement of the impending nuptials, their young hearts filled with dreams of romance and adventure.

Eleanor smiled, the enthusiasm of her sisters infectious. The rooms were abuzz with the preparations for the wedding, with servants—an army of them, kindly provided by Alexander when he found out just how dire their circumstances were—bustling to ensure every detail was attended to. Yet, amid the joyful chaos, a sense of responsibility and duty weighed heavily on her shoulders.

Alexander had also sent a highly sought after seamstress to her, and the woman had just arrived. No doubt her nimble fingers were ready to craft an intricately designed wedding gown from the most luxurious fabrics that would capture the essence of elegance and grace.

Eleanor would soon embark on a journey that would be scrutinized by the highest echelons of society, and her attire would play a significant role in this carefully choreographed performance.

With her sisters beside her, Eleanor met with the seamstress to discuss the details of the wedding dress. They deliberated over fabrics, lace, beading and the most up-to-date fashions. Every step would ensure that the gown would reflect both her personal style and new status. Eleanor would follow the dictates of fashion, but she was determined to retain her individuality.

As they worked on the dress, Olivia was continually drawn to the door to receive more flowers, congratulatory correspondence and gifts. It looked like the ton were ready to believe the engagement story Lady Beatrice had already cleverly circulated.

Lady Beatrice sat with her mother now. Eleanor couldn't wait to hear if she managed a coherent conversation and her opinions about the upcoming wedding of her eldest daughter.

Olivia popped into the room waving a stack of colorful notes. "We have even received a flurry of invitations to pre-wedding events."

Eleanor's life, and that of her sisters, was about to change in profound ways. The manor was alive with excitement and anticipation, but amid it all, questions still echoed in her mind. How would her own journey unfold? What sacrifices would she have to make in the name of family and duty? But Eleanor couldn't falter. Her love for her family and her mother's legacy had prepared her for this moment.

Later that afternoon, as the sun cast long shadows across the manicured gardens of the estate, a knock at the door signaled the arrival of Alexander himself. He was dressed impeccably, exuding the aura of a man who was accustomed to commanding attention and respect in every setting.

Eleanor greeted him in the drawing room, where the scent of freshly blooming flowers lingered in the air. Her sisters retreated to another room to give them privacy.

Alexander smiled warmly. "Your family's home is truly exquisite." His gaze intensified. "It reflects the grace and elegance that I have always associated with you."

Eleanor let out a sigh. "You have visited on many other occasions. Lord Weston, I'm already marrying you. No need to attempt to impress me with your charm."

"So, it is true then?" His smile became charmingly roguish as he closed the distance to Eleanor. "I do still charm you?"

She chose not to answer.

Alexander took a step closer, his gaze unwavering as he spoke earnestly. "I understand the attachment you have to this place—your home—but we must discuss your living arrangements after our marriage."

Eleanor couldn't hide the hesitation in her voice. "I've been thinking about it, and I believe it's best for me to stay here, with my family." It was one of the topics that prevented her from succumbing to sleep easily. "This home has been a part of our family for generations, and I couldn't bear to part with it."

Alexander's expression remained composed, but there was a note of concern in his eyes. "I've organized a comfortable residence for us in my family home, one befitting our station. It's a grand house with all the luxuries you could wish for."

Eleanor glanced up at him, her chin jutting out. "I appreciate your thoughtfulness, Lord Weston, but my family's security and happiness are of utmost importance to me. I simply cannot leave my sisters behind."

Alexander sighed and rolled his shoulders as if readying himself for battle. "I understand your devotion to your family." She could tell he was attempting to be patient, and while she appreciated the effort, it did nothing to change her mind. "It is an admirable quality. But if you stay here, the situation will become increasingly untenable. The ton is relentless, and any further scandal surrounding our engagement and marriage will make it impossible for you and your family to remain in peace."

Eleanor met his gaze firmly, her voice unwavering. "I cannot abandon my sisters, Alexander. We have faced hardships together, and I will not leave them to navigate the treacherous waters of society alone."

Alexander's expression softened, and he took a step closer to her. "I admire your loyalty, Eleanor." He took her hands in his, and she contemplated pulling them away but found she didn't want to. "It is one of the qualities that drew me to you. But I have thought about a solution that could protect your family and allow them to continue living in comfort."

Eleanor regarded him with curiosity. "What solution do you propose?"

"It would be best if your family moved into my residence with us. There, they will be provided with the protection, security, and support they need, while still enjoying the privileges of high society."

Eleanor blinked in surprise. So surprised she found it hard to speak for a for moments. "That's a generous offer. Very generous. But it is too much to ask of you and your grandmother."

Would her sisters agree to move? She had to speak to them first before further discussing his offer.

Alexander squeezed her hands. "I want to see you happy and your family secure. Your happiness is my happiness, and your concerns are my concerns. I will do anything to ensure your well-being."

Eleanor was torn, her heart clenching. She wanted to believe him so badly, but it was difficult. He had let her down before... what were the chances he would again?

"Please excuse my interruption, your ladyship." A young servant entered the drawing room. "The seamstress is ready for you."

"We shall discuss this later." Alexander kissed her knuckles.

Eleanor was rather afraid of exactly that, but she pressed her lips together to keep from saying anything she might later regret. She allowed the servant to lead her away, glad for the reprieve. Alexander was correct—if they didn't live together and behave like perfectly happy newlyweds after the wedding, the ton would be merciless. But confound it, she didn't want to leave her sisters with a mother who could scarcely get out of bed most days.

As she stepped into the room where the seamstress was waiting, Eleanor forced a serene smile onto her face. The seamstress, a skilled woman with years of experience, was ready with the delicate fabrics and lace that would soon transform into her wedding gown.

Eleanor stood on a small platform as the woman worked her magic, carefully measuring and adjusting the materials. It was a moment that should have been filled with excitement and joy, but Eleanor's mind couldn't help but drift to the complexities of her situation.

Without warning, her sisters slipped into the room, their eyes wide with excitement. Mary was the first to speak, her voice barely above a hushed tone. "Eleanor, what will your wedding dress look like?"

She turned her head to smile at her youngest sister. "It will be exquisite, Mary. The seamstress is working diligently to make it perfect."

Olivia chimed in with a more practical question, "And where will you and Lord Weston live after the wedding? Will you be close by?"

Eleanor nodded. "I suppose that depends on Lord Weston."

Caroline couldn't contain her excitement. "Will you carry orchids in your hands when you walk down the aisle like Mama did?"

Eleanor's smile faltered briefly at the question, and she paused before answering. "I haven't thought of that yet."

The sisters exchanged glances.

"Now, run off and ready yourselves," she quickly said. "The seamstress will be working on your dresses after mine, and I expect you all to be on your best behavior."

Mary and Caroline giggled and scampered off, but Olivia remained. Eleanor sighed.

"I am all right, Liv," she promised. "Though, I would like peace to collect my thoughts."

Olivia looked like she wanted to say more, but her eyes shifted to the seamstress. She knew they couldn't speak candidly in the presence of someone else. Olivia nodded before disappearing after her sisters.

It was only then that Eleanor allowed her shoulders to sag. The woman continued her work, and Eleanor was temporarily preoccupied with her thoughts, concerns, and curiosities. She had once dreamed of this day. Accepting a proposal from Alexander, excitedly organizing her wedding with help from her mother and sisters, wearing an exquisite gown. But all of that was before he'd broken her heart. Now that it was happening, she wasn't sure what to think.

As the seamstress molded and pinned the fine fabric around her, Eleanor slumped into her own thoughts. The cards and flowers sent by the ton didn't really mean anything. The real test would be how they treated her after the wedding. Would invitations dry up? Would she receive the cut direct any time she showed her face?

After the fitting, Eleanor walked to the comfort of her family's small sitting room, seeking a moment of respite from the wedding preparations and the complications of her impending marriage to Lord Alexander Weston. As she sat by the window, gazing out at the garden, a footman entered the room to announce a visitor.

"Lord Satterfield, my lady," the footman declared.

Eleanor was taken aback by the unexpected caller. She had not anticipated seeing Lord Satterfield, a man who had known her family for many years and who had often crossed paths with her at social gatherings. But as he entered the room, his expression was grave, and his eyes held a glint of concern.

Eleanor greeted him with a polite nod. "Lord Satterfield, to what do I owe this unexpected visit?"

He approached her with a sense of urgency. "Lady Eleanor, I must speak with you in private. It's a matter of great importance."

Eleanor, intrigued and slightly apprehensive, nodded to the footman, who discreetly exited the room, leaving the door ajar and them in solitude. She motioned for Lord Satterfield to take a seat, her curiosity growing with each passing moment.

He settled into a nearby chair, his gaze remained fixed on Eleanor's face. He began in a solemn tone, "I have heard rumors about your engagement to Lord Weston, and I could not help but feel a sense of unease. I have known you and your family for years, and I've witnessed your kindness and resilience in the face of adversity."

Eleanor furrowed her brow, uncertain where he was leading with his words. "What concerns you, Lord Satterfield?"

He leaned in, his voice barely above a whisper. "Eleanor, I want you to know that if you find yourself in a situation you wish to escape, a situation that is not to your liking, you have an alternative."

Eleanor's gaze sharpened, her curiosity mixed with confusion. "An alternative?"

Lord Satterfield's expression was earnest. "I offer you an alternative, Eleanor. If Weston's marriage proposal is not what you desire, if it's a choice made of necessity rather than love, you have the option to marry me. I would be honored to be the one to save you from a marriage that may not bring you happiness."

Chapter Twelve

Eleanor sat back in her chair, her mind racing as she processed Lord Satterfield's offer. It was an unexpected proposition, one that had the potential to alter the course of her life once again. She had agreed to marry Alexander for the sake of her own and her family's honor, but the prospect of an alternative left her conflicted.

She regarded Lord Satterfield for some moments. She hadn't wanted to marry this man some days ago, and nothing had changed about the way she felt about him. He was a nice man, but one of her father's associates, not her own. And she had made her decision. At least Alexander was the man who'd ruined her in the garden. Marrying him fit the story of a secret engagement and wedding as soon as the mourning period of six months was complete.

She gave the man a polite nod. "Your offer is generous, and I appreciate your concern. However, the decision I have made is not one I take lightly. I am in love with Lord Weston, and I am committed to seeing it through."

Lord Satterfield nodded, accepting her response with a hint of disappointment but also understanding. "I respect your decision, Lady Eleanor. Please know that should you change your mind or find yourself in need of assistance, I am here to offer my support."

Eleanor offered him a small, grateful smile. "Thank you, Lord Satterfield. Your kindness is greatly appreciated."

The older man took his leave, his footsteps echoing faintly in the corridor as he made his way out of the house. She let out a sigh of relief, grateful for his concern, but aware of the potential scandal that would arise from entertaining his offer. She already had to deal with one scandal, thanks to her hurried wedding. The last thing her family needed was her jilting Alexander to marry Lord Satterfield. She would ruin them beyond repair.

As she turned back to the room, she was met with the sight of Alexander, who had just entered. His sharp gaze immediately caught the unease in her expression.

"Eleanor." His tone was on the frosty side. "Why were you secluded in a room with Satterfield. What did he want?"

For a moment, Eleanor hesitated, contemplating how much to reveal. She had never been one to keep secrets, but the complications of her situation demanded discretion. She opted for caution. "He came to offer his support, and to express his concern about our impending marriage."

Alexander's brow furrowed, and he moved closer to her. "Concern about our marriage? What the hell does that mean?"

Eleanor hesitated once more, aware that explaining the full extent of Lord Satterfield's offer would only lead to more questions and potential complications. "He had heard the rumors, and fears that we are not marrying for love."

Alexander's frustration was palpable as he crossed his arms, his gaze intense. "And what do you believe, Eleanor? Do you agree with his sentiment?"

Eleanor met his gaze evenly. "I believe that our situation is complicated, and my duty to my family is of utmost importance. Following the events of last night, marrying you is the path I have chosen."

As the tension in the room escalated, Alexander's frustration reached its peak. He stepped closer to her, his voice edged with anger. "Eleanor, tell me the truth. What was that man here for? I know it's more than just to vocalize his concern. The only person he has ever been concerned about is himself."

Eleanor met his gaze with a mixture of reluctance and determination. "He offered me an alternative, Alexander."

His eyes flared with fury, and he clenched his fists. "An alternative? What kind of alternative?"

Anger emanated from him, and Eleanor stepped closer to Alexander to try to defuse the situation. "Alexander, there's no need for anger or threats. I refused his offer, and that's the end of it."

But her new fiancé seemed beyond reason. The mere idea that someone, no doubt especially Lord Satterfield, as there seemed to be some personal animosity between them, had dared to offer an alternative proposal clearly incensed him. She shouldn't have allowed Alexander to push her so much that she revealed it. Too late to change that now.

"He deserves to be challenged," Alexander spluttered. "I'll find him and kill him. No one propositions my wife. No one."

Eleanor's eyes widened, and she grabbed his arm to stop him from behaving recklessly. "No, Alexander, you must not. That would only lead to more scandal and trouble." She stood in his way. "I'm not your wife, by the way. I'm still your betrothed."

"Semantics." He turned to face her, his anger unabated. "You belong to me whether you like it or not." She didn't understand why he was being so possessive. She had never seen this side to him before. "I will not allow anyone to insult you or question our union."

Eleanor glared at him, her voice firm. "You must trust me, Alexander. I handled the situation, and Lord Satterfield is aware that my decision is final. There is no need for violence or ruining my family further."

Alexander took a step back, though he still seethed with anger. At least he was starting to listen. "Fine, but he and anyone else must understand that you belong to me now. Any such proposals are a grave insult to me, and there will be consequences."

Eleanor was not one to back down from a confrontation. She met his threat with a question of her own. "Does that mean I have the same right, Alexander?"

He lifted his brow as if perplexed. "What do you mean?"

Eleanor's voice turned steely as she confronted him with a painful memory. "I remember a different story when I caught you with Abigail. Should there have been consequences then?"

She didn't understand why she'd even brought it up, but his anger ignited hers, and for once, she couldn't seem to control the words as they flew out of her mouth.

Alexander's face turned stoney. "There were," he said. "I lost you."

Eleanor's heart squeezed. It was her fault for even bringing it up, and now, she had to deal with her swirling emotions.

"I must check on my sisters." Head held high, Eleanor turned and left the room.

She needed time and space to collect her thoughts and emotions.

The grand day had arrived, the day of Eleanor's wedding to Lord Alexander Weston. The manor was abuzz with preparations, and in her chambers, the atmosphere was filled with both excitement and a sense of finality. Eleanor's three sisters, Olivia, Caroline, and Mary, flitted around her like delicate butterflies, ensuring every detail was just right.

Eleanor sat at her vanity, clad in her undergarments as her sisters fussed over her. Olivia attended to her hair. Caroline oversaw the voluminous skirts of the wedding gown, while Mary provided her with comforting words and adoring glances.

Mary carefully secured Eleanor's veil, her voice filled with sisterly affection. "You look positively radiant, Ellie, Lord Weston is a lucky man."

Caroline chimed in, her eyes shining with excitement, "I cannot believe you are getting married! This is like a dream come true."

"Are you happy, though?" Olivia watched Eleanor with a touch of worry. "Truly happy?"

Eleanor met Olivia's reflection in the mirror and offered a tender smile. "Yes, I am." This wasn't a lie. While she wasn't pleased about marrying Alexander, it could be much worse. She convinced him to stay in her family home for the time being, which meant she didn't have to leave her sisters or her mother. "This is what is best for us, for our family. Lord Weston is a good man, and I believe this union will secure our future."

Mary nodded in agreement, her touch gentle as she adjusted a stray strand of hair. "You are a remarkable sister, Eleanor," she said. "Your strength and selflessness inspire us all."

The final touch was completed as they secured a delicate bouquet of fresh white roses in Eleanor's hand, a symbol of and purity. The sisters took a step back, admiring the beautiful bride before them.

As Eleanor rose from her seat, her sisters gathered around her, their expressions a mix of joy and melancholy. Caroline blinked back tears, and Mary clung to her sister's hand.

Eleanor's heart swelled with love for her sisters, the three constants in her life. "I will always be there for you, my dears. This is a new chapter for us, but our bond will remain unbreakable."

With a last shared embrace, Eleanor made her way to the door, the girls following behind. They descended the grand staircase of the manor, the wedding march playing softly in the background.

Outside, the sun shone brightly, casting a warm glow over the garden where the wedding would take place. Alexander awaited her at the altar, his expression a mix of anticipation and genuine affection.

As she stepped out into the garden, Eleanor's heart swelled with emotion. The garden provided a picturesque setting for the ceremony, bathed in the soft hues of twilight. Eleanor, resplendent in her bridal attire, walked down the garden path with her three younger sisters by her side. In a touching tribute to their late father, a white rose adorned an empty chair, a symbol of his enduring presence in their hearts.

Her heart ached with a bittersweet longing. Mother had tried so hard to get up, help with the preparations, and attend today, but the effort brought on a collapse, which their doctor was unable to diagnose. Her mother's absence left an unmistakable void, a feeling of incompleteness that cast a shadow over the otherwise joy-filled occasion.

At the altar, Lord Alexander Weston, the embodiment of anticipation and devotion, waited for Eleanor. She arrived by his side, and her sisters offered loving smiles of encouragement before taking their seats.

Alexander had agreed to the family reverend so Eleanor would have another friendly face at the altar. Another kindness from her soon to be husband. The minister began the ceremony with a gentle, solemn tone, setting the scene for the union about to take place. His words filled the air with a sense of reverence as he united the couple in matrimony.

The vows exchanged between Eleanor and Alexander were heartfelt and deeply meaningful, and for a second, Eleanor could swear this was real.

As the ceremony reached its climax, the officiant's voice rose in significance. "By the power vested in me, and in the presence of this assembly of witnesses, I now pronounce you husband and wife."

Eleanor and Alexander locked eyes, their expressions filled with a profound sense of commitment and promise. In that poignant moment, as the sun dipped below the horizon and the garden seemed to hold its breath, Alexander leaned in and tenderly kissed Eleanor, sealing their union as husband and wife.

The garden came to life with applause and joy as the newlyweds shared their first kiss. It was a moment of profound happiness, marking the beginning of a new chapter.

What that chapter was filled with, Eleanor didn't know. But for now, her family was free from scandal...and that was what mattered.

Chapter Thirteen

The intimate reception unfolded in the glow of flickering candlelight casting a warm ambiance over the gathered guests. Soft strains of music floated through the air as Eleanor and Alexander took to the center of the room for their first dance as husband and wife. The delicate lace of Eleanor's gown brushed against the ballroom floor, and the subtle fragrance of fresh flowers mingled with the sweet notes of the music. As they moved together, the dance seemed to encapsulate the essence of a genuine celebration of love.

The servants had done themselves proud in a short period of time, and the room was adorned with floral arrangements and elegant decorations. Tables draped in pristine white linens held crystal glasses, and the soft glow of candlelight reflected in the polished silverware. Laughter and the tinkling sound of glasses being raised in toasts filled the air, creating an atmosphere of conviviality and genuine happiness.

Eleanor stole glances at Alexander's eyes, finding an unspoken understanding between them. Their dance became a silent dialogue, each step a promise and each gaze an affirmation of their shared journey. The guests, caught up in the enchantment of the moment, looked on with smiles that mirrored the newlyweds' joy.

No one uttered words to try to hurt her, though that could be because Lady Beatrice invited influential members of the ton with a sense of loyalty to her.

By the time most of the guests departed, Eleanor couldn't help but feel a profound sense of gratitude for the love that surrounded her.

Alexander's grandmother rose gracefully from her seat, a glint of mischief in her eyes as she approached Eleanor's sisters. "Come along, dears. It's time for us to leave the newlyweds in peace." Her voice carried an air of authority that left no room for protest.

Mary, roused from her gentle slumber, rubbed her eyes and looked around in confusion. Caroline, struggling to keep her eyes open, blinked rapidly, and Olivia, appearing somewhat bored, perked up at the prospect of something new. Beatrice extended her hand to Mary, guiding her with a gentle touch.

Eleanor bent down to kiss Mary's forehead, her voice a soft murmur. "Goodnight, sweet sister. Sleep well."

Mary, still half asleep, mumbled a drowsy response.

Eleanor turned to Caroline, enveloping her in a warm embrace. "Rest, Caroline, we have a big day ahead tomorrow.

This elicited a tired but content smile from her second sister.

Eleanor gave Olivia a playful smile. "Be on your best behavior, Livy. And before you ask, I'm fine. I promise."

Olivia responded with and exaggerated eyeroll, but with her sisters in the capable hands of Beatrice, Eleanor turned her attention back to Alexander. His gaze held a mixture of affection and amusement as they watched the trio depart.

Eleanor offered her gratitude with a sincere smile. "Thank you, Lady Beatrice."

The older woman waved away Eleanor's thanks. "No need for thanks, my dear. It's a pleasure to welcome you officially into the family." Her eyes twinkled. "Now, enjoy your night. We'll take care of the rest."

As the door closed behind Beatrice and the girls, Alexander turned to Eleanor with a mischievous glint in his eyes. "Shall we continue our celebration, Lady Weston?" He tugged her hand to lead her back into the heart of the home.

Lady Weston.

A shiver slid down her spine at the sound of her new name from his lips.

She'd dreamed of being Lady Weston until –

But no, she wouldn't think about that now.

With her nerves fluttering just beneath the surface, she felt the weight of their impending wedding night settle upon her shoulders, a heavy apprehension she couldn't shake. Glancing at Alexander, she searched for reassurance in his eyes.

He noticed the subtle shift in her demeanor and squeezed her hand reassuringly. "No need for nerves. Tonight is about us, about our beginning." His tone was gentle, and as comforting as she had hoped for. "Whatever you're feeling, I promise you it's normal."

She nodded, grateful for his understanding, and let him lead her back into the warmth of the home. The flickering candlelight bathed their surroundings in a soft glow, crafting an intimate atmosphere that mirrored the emotions swirling within Eleanor.

They stepped into her bedroom, and Alexander closed the door behind them, shutting out the noise of the outside world.

Eleanor's heart raced. Her limbs trembled so much, surely he would notice. She couldn't bear him to see her like this. So uncertain, so afraid. She faced Alexander uncertainly, but his gaze held both tenderness and affection, a silent assurance that their connection transcended any uncertainties.

"Alexander," she whispered. It was all she could manage. "I appreciate your patience. Tonight is... it's a lot, and I am not entirely sure—"

He interrupted her, gently touching his fingertip to her lips. "We do not have to do anything you are not ready for."

She pulled away from his touch. "But we do. I cannot risk anyone finding out that we have not... I mean, that we did not." Her cheeks burned, but somehow, she continued, "This must be real. The servants already proved they will talk. I need the rumors to stop, to die down long enough for my sisters to secure a match. Then—"

"I never thought I would see the day when Lady Eleanor was so nervous."

"I am not—" She stopped. No point in denying the obvious. "I have never done this before. And I do not know what to expect."

"I will take care of you," he said. "I promise."

Eleanor hated those words from him.

His promises were always lies.

She knew better than to believe him, but her heart wanted to. So badly.

"Shall I show you to your rooms?" Eleanor swallowed. "Before we..." She couldn't finish the sentence.

Alexander shook his head, a determined glint in his eyes. "We will share a room. We are husband and wife now, and I don't want to start our marriage apart. Even if it is the customary thing to do."

A mixture of emotions flickered through Eleanor's head and probably across her face as well. This wasn't what she expected. She didn't know much about physical intimacy between husband and wife, but spending the whole night, every night, so close to her new husband sounded so much more taxing than anything she had imagined.

She felt an urgent need to explain herself to him. "I do not how I want to start our marriage. I am unsure how to navigate this." She gestured between them. "Whatever this is, it is not a real marriage. It's not like we have feelings for one another." Her heart rebelled at the blatant lie, but she powered on, "This marriage is for appearances, to save my reputation."

Alexander reached for her hand and pulled her knuckles to his mouth. "Keep telling yourself that, Eleanor. And maybe for you, it is not. But for me, this marriage is real."

"Stop it." She snatched back her hand. "Stop saying things like that."

"I will not. I won't lie to you. We can go at whatever pace you are comfortable with. There is no rush. But I want to be close to you tonight. You are my wife, my brand-new wife, and I am allowed to do that." He took a step towards her. "I am going to kiss you now."

Eleanor wanted to tell him not to. She wanted to push him away and insist he go to his own rooms, but she was powerless against him. To be fair, she was powerless against her own desire.

He kissed her, slowly, sensuously. He brushed his lips over hers. Her skin heated, and everywhere he touched her tingled. She felt sparks between them, and suddenly their wedding seemed real in a way she hadn't expected. His hands moved around her waist and pulled her closer to him as their kiss deepened. She felt the heat of his body through the fabric of her dress, and it caused a flurry of sensations to dance up and down her spine.

His touch was gentle yet firm, sending a thrill of pleasure throughout Eleanor's body. Without thinking, she wrapped her arms around Alexander's neck as he held her close, their mouths melding together in perfect harmony. Every inch of Eleanor's body ached for him, every nerve ending vibrating with an intoxicating mix of frustration and desire. Finally, after what seemed like ages, Alexander released Eleanor from his embrace and stepped back.

Eleanor's trembling fingers brushed against her lips as Alexander gazed at her with an unmistakable sense of possession. The intensity in his eyes ignited a fierce heat within her body.

"Turn around." The command in his tone was evident.

She hated how docile she was being, but couldn't help it. She turned her back to him.

He moved so close, his breath tickled the back of her neck. Slowly, he began to unlace her wedding gown.

Eleanor closed her eyes and let out a shaky breath. How could she handle this? Her brain was screaming for her to resist, to turn around and push him away like she'd done so many times before. But her heart clamored for more. It felt so good to be in his arms again.

The bodice of her dress fell to the floor, exposing her corset. Alexander gently pulled the lace fabric of her camisole down over her shoulder. His fingers brushed her skin, his touch sending shivers through her body. Eleanor held her breath as he unlaced the corset that held her petticoats in place.

Eleanor's cheeks burned with shame and desire as the corset fell to the floor. Now she was clad in only her chemise. Alexander's eyes never wavered from hers as he began to strip that away from her too.

It wasn't long before she was completely bare in front of him.

Her first instinct was to reach up and cross her arms over her bare breasts, but Alexander stopped her.

"Don't," he said. "Do not hide yourself from me."

Eleanor stood still as Alexander's eyes roamed over her body, taking in her every curve. She clenched her hands at her sides. She'd never be so exposed, so vulnerable as she was right now, but she didn't move. She let him look… she had nothing to be ashamed of.

"You are so beautiful." He took a step back, his gaze flicking up to meet hers.

Eleanor looked away, embarrassed and confused. As much as she wanted him to gaze upon her, she couldn't stand it when he did.

"Do not look away, Eleanor," he said. "I will not do anything you don't want me to, but I want you to look at me. I want you to let me see you."

Eleanor forced herself to meet his gaze, but she couldn't keep her eyes on his. She stared at his chin, his neck, anywhere but his eyes.

"Look at me." The commanding tone was back.

His tone sent a tremor through Eleanor's body, one that spread slowly from her head to her toes. She felt too vulnerable standing before him, but the expression in Alexander's eyes was so intoxicating that she couldn't bring herself to be embarrassed.

Questions about what was happening between them, why he was doing this again, why he was so intent on ravaging her and ruining her life, circled in her brain. But the heat coursing through her body was turning her into a mass of quivering need.

Alexander pulled Eleanor close to him again, his hands running over her back as their lips met once more. As they kissed, the heat of her desire rose to meet his body as if they were melding together.

He wrapped his arms around her, holding her against him as he traced the outline of her ear with his tongue. Waves of pleasure crashed over her. She let her eyes flutter shut, her heart thudding in her chest as she struggled to get her breathing under control.

He leaned forward, kissing her shoulder as he cupped her breasts in his hands. No doubt he felt her nipples hardening under his touch. Her desire amped up several notches. She'd denied her desire for him for so long, and now she couldn't get enough of him.

Alexander kissed the nape of her neck as he walked her over to the bed.

There was no going back now.

And honestly?

She didn't want to.

<h1 style="text-align:center; font-style:italic;">Chapter Fourteen</h1>

Alexander couldn't stop staring. He always knew Eleanor would be a vision once he finally stripped her bare, but he never thought she'd render him completely speechless. Her breasts filled his hands, and he couldn't wait to take each one between his lips.

He laid her on the bed. Her eyes were wide, full of vulnerability and uncertainty. She was a virgin, pure and innocent. His body trembled at the thought of claiming her.

She was his now.

She would always be his.

Her arms were clutched to her chest, though she hadn't hidden her shaking hands.

Alexander moved towards her, reaching up to touch her cheek with his fingertips. "Relax," he whispered. "I will not hurt you. I promise."

Eleanor closed her eyes as Alexander kissed her forehead, her cheeks, her nose. A soft sigh slipped from between her lips, and Alexander felt himself grow harder than he thought possible.

He brushed her hair back away from her face, his fingers sliding over her neck and collarbone.

Eleanor's chest rose and fell in quick breaths as Alexander covered her shoulder with kisses, his hands skimming up her arms and brushing her hair back off her face.

He wrapped his lips around one of her nipples, and Eleanor's body quivered. Alexander held her closer to him, sucking and teasing her with his tongue.

She moaned, and he had to hold himself back from taking her right then.

He kissed his way over the curve of her breast and toward her other nipple. He smiled as Eleanor let out a cute gasp of surprise when his lips closed around the sensitive peak.

With luck, he would spend the rest of the night lavishing attention on Eleanor's body.

Alexander never imagined she would respond so enthusiastically. He coaxed her body open to him, and soon she was falling apart in his arms. Beneath his fingers and his lips, she was wild and passionate. She didn't hide herself from him. In fact, she gave him everything he wanted, everything he asked for. And he loved her for it.

He traced his fingertips down her body, laying a trail of kisses over her ribcage, her belly.

Eleanor's head rolled back and forth on the bed as Alexander kissed her inner thigh. Her breathing was heavy, no doubt she was trying to stay quiet. He wanted her to call out to him, to scream and moan.

She let out a low groan, and Alexander smiled as he moved closer to her center. He kissed her there, his tongue dancing circles around her clit.

Eleanor's hips bucked off the bed, and she called out his name, still clutching the sheet in her trembling hands. "Alexander," she said again, her voice barely a whisper.

He looked up to find Eleanor's eyes closed and her face flushed red with pleasure. The sight made him hungry for more of her, so he lowered himself down to kiss and lick every inch of her body.

She clutched his hair, and he groaned, his lips pressed against her mound.

He needed this.

He needed her.

She tasted delicious, like nectar from the fruits only the gods possessed.

His tongue darted in and out of her, teasing her and flicking against her.

"Alexander. She lifted her hips from the bed in search of more, and he gave it to her.

Her body tightened around him in an instant, her orgasm building. Had he ever felt anything as amazing as Eleanor's body as it began to shake? She gripped his hair as she called out his name again.

He continued to work her with his lips and tongue, sending her over the edge.

It only took a few moments before she exploded in his mouth, her juices spilling over his tongue.

Her body relaxed again, and Alexander climbed up her body, kissing her lips and taking her into his arms.

"What...what was that?" she asked, breathless, her voice barely more than a whisper.

"The beginning." Alexander smiled against her soft skin. "We've got all night, and I intend to use every second of it."

He feathered soft kisses to her neck, her shoulder, her cheek.

"I want you," she whispered.

Alexander gazed into her face. "I've wanted you since the moment I met you.

She traced her fingertips over his back, her nails raking over his flesh. He hissed in pleasure as she pulled him closer to her, pressing her lips against his neck.

"Please, Alexander," she whispered, and it was nearly his undoing.

He quickly shed his clothing until he was just as bare as she. Crawling on top of her, he couldn't take his eyes off her beautiful face.

"I expect this will hurt," he told her, "But I've prepared you. It should lessen the pain. But I promise, Eleanor... I promise it will be worth it."

She bit her bottom lip but nodded, trusting him.

He wasn't sure he had earned her trust, but it didn't matter. He had it, and that was all that mattered.

He entered her excruciatingly slowly, and Eleanor winced in pain, her teeth digging into her bottom lip. He knew the feeling, the pain that accompanied the loss of innocence.

He kissed her as he pushed himself inside her. He kept his gaze on her, watching every change that played over her face. He could almost read her thoughts, and he held her close to him, watching her eyes as he moved his cock deeper into her warmth.

She was so warm, so tight, and he groaned. It took every ounce of self-control in him to maintain this slow, arduous pace. He wanted to take her, to fill her to the brink, stretch her slick walls as far as they could go, and then push her even farther, but he held back.

Barely.

Eleanor groaned as well while he filled her, her hips rising to meet him.

He stopped as her body tensed, and he leaned forward to kiss her.

"I'm fine," she breathed, her eyes wide. "Please don't stop."

He moved inside her again, filling her with his body. Hot, consuming waves crashed through him, and he never wanted to let her go.

He wanted to spend the rest of his life inside her, spilling his seed so they had children, growing old and holding her as they watched their grandchildren play.

The thought of having a family with her filled him with joy, ecstasy, and love.

It fueled him, and he started thrusting faster. She moaned under him, her hips rolling with his.

She slid her hands up and down his back, and Alexander had to close his eyes and fight the sensation. He wanted to see her face as the pleasure tore through her.

For the first time in his life, he wanted to watch someone come undone.

He wanted to see the pleasure, the ecstasy that played over her face. Wanted to watch Eleanor climax so hard she saw stars. Because of him.

He pushed himself inside her, his cock sliding in and out of her slick walls.

She dug her fingernails into his back, and she bit her lip, trying to hold back her cries.

She was beautiful, and he wanted to show her just how beautiful she was to him.

He wanted to make her scream.

She traced her hands over his chest, her nails scratching him lightly as her body tensed again, and then she was shaking underneath him.

Alexander quickened his pace, staying with her as she came undone.

Eleanor's body convulsed underneath him, and Alexander felt a warm rush of tears spilling from her eyes.

He wanted to be there for her, to hold her and tell her everything would be all right. He wanted to show her the truth of how much he cared for her.

Alexander pushed deeper inside her, her body shivering against his as she squeezed him with her muscles. They moved as one, slowly at first, building in speed until Alexander pounded into her.

He wrapped his fingers in her hair and pulled her head back, exposing her neck.

He wanted to make her his, to brand her, and he kissed her neck with more force.

"Alexander!" she called out, her voice husky and weak.

His seed spilled inside her, filling her tight, slick walls. His body convulsed against hers, and when his release finally subsided, he rested his forehead on her shoulder.

Eleanor's breath came in heaving pants, and he slid off her. He lay on his side next to her and wrapped his arms around her, holding her close to him.

"Are you all right?" he asked.

Eleanor nodded, though she said nothing.

Alexander kissed her cheek and smiled down at her. "I will take that as a yes." He stared into her beautiful eyes. "Are you hurt?"

She shook her head. "No. I mean, I am sore, but…I don't know. It hurt, but I kind of liked it."

Alexander laughed. "You enjoyed being ravished?"

Eleanor laughed as well. "No, not exactly." She glanced at him through her lashes. "Well, perhaps. It just made me feel…"

"Tell me."

"Normal. You made me feel normal. Our bodies fit together. I felt like I belonged with you." She shook her head. "I apologize. I don't know what I am saying. I am not thinking properly."

Alexander kissed her on the lips, unable to express what she was making him feel. He wanted to tell her that she was everything he ever wanted or needed, but he had to be careful.

He couldn't lose her. She was the prize, and there would be a war for her.

But it didn't matter.

He had made a mistake in their past, and he would do everything in his power to make up for that, to make her fall back in love with him. No matter what it took.

He could do it. He had to.

Eleanor sighed, their naked bodies pressed against each other, and he smiled.

They would be fine, and then he would find a way to make her love him again.

Her brow furrowed as if deep in thought. "What?" he asked gently. "What is it?"

"It's just..." She looked away. "Does it always feel like that?"

Alexander was silent for a long moment. There were so many things he wanted to say, so many things he wanted to tell her, but he couldn't find the right words. The only thing that came to him was the truth. Nothing flowery. Nothing poetic. Just the simple truth. "No," he finally said. "No, it doesn't."

Chapter Fifteen

As the soft morning light filtered through the curtains, Eleanor stirred. She blinked her eyes open, a sense of tranquility washing over her as she became aware of her peaceful surroundings.

She stretched, and a pleasant soreness in her muscles reminded her of the previous day's celebrations and the comforting warmth of shared moments. Her gaze shifted to the figure beside her, and a tender smile curved her lips. Alexander lay there peacefully, his features relaxed in the morning light, his rhythmic breathing a soothing melody.

The weight of the night was a distant memory, replaced by the comfort of a restful sleep. For the first time in what felt like an eternity, a sense of calm settled within her. There was a comfort in waking up next to Alexander, a warmth she hadn't anticipated.

She watched him sleep for a moment, his presence oddly reassuring, and Eleanor couldn't help but appreciate the serenity of the morning, a peaceful contrast to the whirlwind events leading to their union.

With a soft sigh, she shifted, feeling the contentment seep into her bones. The bed felt different, cozier, and for the first time, she realized how exhausted she had been, both physically and emotionally. The embrace of slumber in Alexander's presence was a welcome respite from the worries that had consumed her in recent times.

As she glanced around the room, memories of their wedding day flooded back—her sisters' joyful faces, the laughter, the dancing. It had been a day of union and celebration despite the uncertainties that lingered in the corners of her mind.

Eleanor stole another glance at Alexander, cherishing the quiet intimacy of the moment. She couldn't deny the sense of ease that had settled between them during the night. The worries and fears she had carried seemed distant in the soft light of the morning, replaced by a sense of possibility.

With a gentle stretch, Eleanor slowly sat up, careful not to disturb Alexander's peace. She took a deep breath, relishing the newfound tranquility and the promise of a new beginning. The morning held a different kind of hope, a sense of companionship that she hadn't expected.

"You are staring, wife," Alexander murmured with his eyes still closed.

"Don't call me that." She scowled at him.

"But isn't that what you are?" he asked, opening one eye.

"Yes, but–" She was flustered. Back to being that uncertain, vulnerable woman from last night.

"You are my wife, Eleanor." He narrowed his eyes. "Why are you flushed?"

"What are you talking about?"

The heat under her skin deepened. He lifted on one elbow. "You want to do it again?"

Again? Did she? Even if she did, she certainly couldn't say so out loud. "What? No–"

"You're a terrible liar."

Eleanor sighed. Yes, she was. Her sisters always teased her about it.

"Tell me," He said. "I want to hear you say what you want."

He kissed her neck slowly, lapping his tongue in small circles. Her eyes rolled back, and the memories of last night came to her in a rush.

"Tell me. I need to hear you say it."

She shook her head and tried to get out of bed.

He grabbed her wrist and pulled her on top of him. "I'm waiting."

She didn't want to tell him. She didn't want to give in. But it was difficult to resist him, and even harder to resist her own desire.

She sighed again, slumped in resignation. "I want...you."

He caressed her back, his touch making her shudder with pleasure. Heat bloomed between her legs, and she tightened around him as the softness of her breasts pressed into his hard muscles.

"Tell me what you want. What do you long for? Tell me. I'll give you anything."

He would, she knew that. Despite everything, Alexander would keep his word. Her lips trembled, and she felt the current of some unnamed emotion inside her. She had never felt like this before, and it was terrifying.

At the back of her mind, she knew that she should resist even though her body longed for him. But her mouth moved on its own, and she whispered, "I want to do it again."

His hardness pressed against her thigh, and desire flared in his gaze. This need was something she couldn't explain but she craved. She had only connected with him once, and already she craved it again. What was happening to her?

"There's so much I want to show you." He pulled away. "But I want you to feel it too." He shifted, his hands on her waist as she straddled him.

His cock pressed against her. He wanted her just as much as she wanted him.

"Please." She didn't know what she was asking for. She didn't know what happened to her when she was with him. All she knew was that she wanted him inside her.

He grabbed his cock with one hand and lifted her with the other. He guided her along his dick until he pushed himself deeper inside, and moments later, he was thrusting into her, harder and faster.

The pleasure of him filling her was so great that her mind felt like it was about to burst, and Eleanor moaned in his mouth.

"You are so tight," he groaned, his lips on her neck. "So fucking tight."

It was a curse and a compliment at the same time, but she didn't care. She didn't know why, but she wanted him to take her like this, much rougher than the night before. There would be bruises on her skin, marks on her neck, and she would revel in the possession of it all. Something wicked had come over her, but she was too far gone to care.

"Touch yourself." Alexander said.

Eleanor opened her eyes. "I don't know how."

He guided her hand to one of her breasts, and she moaned out. "Touch your breast. I want to see you play with it."

Eleanor did as he said and gave each nipple a tweak. She moaned in pleasure, and Alexander groaned as well.

"Touch yourself," he said. "I want to watch you come."

Again, she obeyed him, even though she wasn't sure what to do. Her head rolled back, and she groaned as she felt herself getting closer.

Alexander grabbed both her hips. "I want to taste you. Touch yourself, and I'll make you come."

He lifted her from his cock and moved her, supporting her so she was nearly sitting on his face.

She was exposed. Totally bare. "Alexander, wait..."

"Trust me," he murmured before sliding his tongue along her slit.

Eleanor gasped and had to move her hands away to keep herself from falling over. She felt his tongue against her, and she moaned out as he began to lick her. He was a skilled, experienced lover, and it showed.

She had never even considered something like this before, and yet she was already dripping wet. Pressure was building inside her, and she almost came when his tongue flicked against her clit.

Eleanor sucked in a tight breath, barely able to stay in position as he began to tease her clit with his tongue. He flicked it slowly before parting her lips. He licked along her slit and sucked lightly on her core. He grabbed her cheeks firmly, but lightly enough to not hurt.

She hadn't expected this. Eleanor moaned out loud as she felt her climax building.

Alexander groaned as he lapped at her wetness. "Your pussy is so sweet." He glanced up at her. "It tastes divine."

Eleanor shuddered at his words. Her eyes were locked onto his, and she felt completely exposed in his gaze.

She moaned, grinding herself wantonly against his face. He moved his tongue inside her, teasing an especially sensitive spot. Her core tightened, and she groaned, though whether it with pain or pleasure, she couldn't say.

"You're so close, aren't you?" he asked.

She nodded, unable to see what he was doing with her.

"Come for me. Come on my face."

Alexander slid his tongue against her, and her body responded immediately. Her clit throbbed as he caressed it. She was about to explode. She cried out as her orgasm washed over her.

Her body tremored as her orgasm began to subside, and her eyes moved to Alexander. He was staring at her, his eyes focused on her body.

"Alexander." Her heart raced while her mind reeled from what had just happened. Alexander sat up and took her in his arms. His hardness pressed against her thigh, and she wanted more. She wanted this again and again. "I want you."

He pressed himself against her. "Do you trust me?"

She nodded, unable to form any words.

He eased her on her stomach, and she held herself up with her hands. He trailed his fingers over her behind like she was something holy.

"Fuck, your body is beautiful," he said.

He spread her legs further apart and began to push himself into her. Eleanor groaned in pleasure as he filled her, and she buried her face in the sheets as she clenched her fists around them. Alexander's hard cock was deep inside her, another orgasm building.

"Touch yourself until you come."

Eleanor listened to his words, and her hands moved down to her crotch. The pleasure was so great that she almost came.

"How does it feel?" he asked.

She couldn't speak. All she could do was moan. But he seemed to understand her. He thrust in hard, his hips slapping against her butt, and she moaned out.

"Do you like it?" he asked.

Eleanor nodded.

"Good," he said. "I want you to come again."

He began to thrust harder, and she kept pace with him.

"I want you so filled with my seed, it drips out of you hours from now."

Another orgasm built. She rubbed herself faster as she pressed her face into the sheets. Alexander reached around her and squeezed her breasts as he fucked her.

"I'm going to come," he said, his voice tight.

His fingers slipped underneath her, and he pinched her nipples. Her orgasm crashed over her, and she moaned out as her cunt tightened around his cock. He thrust into her a few more times before she felt his length thicken inside her.

His cock began to soften. Eleanor whimpered as he pulled out, but at the same time, he pulled her into his arms.

"We do not have to rise just now," he said. "You can bathe later. I want to smell myself on you."

He pulled the sheets and blankets over her, and Eleanor sighed. This marriage was barely a day old and already much more than she anticipated, and the truth was, she enjoyed it.

She enjoyed it far too much. And that scared her more than anything.

Chapter Sixteen

Alexander savored the tranquility of the morning as he strolled through the estate's gardens, the crisp air refreshing against his skin. It had been a month since his union with Eleanor, a whirlwind of emotions and newfound connections that exceeded his expectations.

Thankfully, Eleanor had agreed to move into his home. This visit to Westonleigh Park gave them a chance to escape the gossips in London and make a few necessary alterations in his London home to accommodate Eleanor, her sisters and her mother.

The estate was abuzz with life, Eleanor's sisters adding a new vitality that he had never experienced as an only child.

He relished those moments with the young ladies, observing their playful banter and the warmth they brought to the household. Olivia's spirited conversations, Caroline's earnest inquiries, and Mary's innocent curiosity—each held a unique charm. It was a revelation to him, so accustomed to solitude during his own childhood, to witness the camaraderie and affection between siblings.

Yet it was the stolen moments alone with Eleanor that Alexander treasured most. Their quiet conversations, the shared laughter and stolen glances, the gradual weaving of their lives into a tapestry of shared experiences, and the newfound ease that seemed to envelop them when alone—it was a revelation, a bond he had yearned for but hadn't anticipated so quickly.

He smiled as he walked. Eleanor's strength and resilience were admirable, the way she carried herself with grace and determination an inspiration. The weight of responsibility hadn't lessened, but there was a sense of shared burden between them, a unity in facing the challenges that lay ahead.

Eleanor's presence had seamlessly woven itself into the fabric of his life. The mornings together were now his sanctuary. Their conversations were varied, sometimes light-hearted and playful, at other times introspective and laden with shared worries. But in every exchange, Alexander found a depth in Eleanor that intrigued him—a depth he longed to explore further.

Alexander paused by a rose bush, one of his mother's favorites, and bent to inhale the delicate fragrance and admire the red petals kissed by morning dew. He turned back toward the house, his heart unexpectedly full. His marriage had filled a void he hadn't realized existed.

He quickened his pace, eager to return to the sanctuary of their shared space. But when he stepped into the foyer, he found Olivia and Caroline embroiled in a heated discussion, their gestures animated and voices rising. Mary hovered nearby, her hands clenched together, a concerned expression etched across her face.

Determined to grasp the cause of the dispute and resolve it before the girls disturbed Eleanor, Alexander approached them. "What's going on?"

Before anyone could respond, Eleanor appeared in the hallway, gliding effortlessly into the scene. "It's nothing for you to worry about, Alexander." With a small smile, she handed him a bundle of notes and letters. "Your mail was inadvertently delivered to me during your walk."

He accepted the letters, noting Eleanor's demeanor. There was a subtle shift in her expression—a blend of her usual warmth laced with caution—as if she were protecting something, perhaps shielding him from unnecessary concerns.

"Thank you." He glanced at the stack before returning his attention to the sisters.

Caroline tried to continue her argument. "But she–"

Eleanor subtly intervened, redirecting their attention. " Let's not dwell on this now. Accompany me for a stroll in the gardens? It's a lovely morning."

The diversion worked, and the sisters obediently followed Eleanor's lead, their bickering now replaced by more amiable chatter. Alexander watched them leave, a faint smile tugging at his lips. Eleanor had a way of diffusing tension effortlessly. There was a certain harmony in the way she handled situations, an innate ability to navigate family affairs with grace and composure.

Alexander made his way to his study, sat at his desk, and sifted through the stack of letters, most appeared routine—invitations, business inquiries, and the like.

His breath hitched. He dropped the routine correspondence as if it burned his skin. In shaking hands, he lifted a letter to read his name and address in elegant script.

A blob of red wax sealed the envelope shut, but he didn't need to see the name of the writer. For a fleeting moment, time seemed to stand still.

He shook himself free of the turmoil whirling in his head.

Perhaps he shouldn't read the damn thing at all. He wanted nothing to do with the woman and had told her so many times. But he couldn't have her contacting Eleanor, which she might do if he ignored her.

With a resigned sigh, he broke the seal with a letter opener and unfolded the message.

Should he confide in Eleanor, seek solace in her company? He didn't want lies and secrets in his marriage. Yet, the weight of his history with the sender held him back, ensnaring him in a labyrinth of hesitation and uncertainty. His relationship with Eleanor was progressing so much better than he had hoped. She wasn't in love with him, not yet, but she would be eventually. He knew it. If he had just a little more time, she would fall for him again just like she had in her first season.

But if she saw this letter, she would never give him a chance.

And honestly? He wouldn't blame her.

The breakfast bell rang, a welcome distraction. He refolded the letter and carefully tucked it away in his desk. He'd contemplate what to do about it later.

He made his way to the breakfast room with his thoughts a whirlwind of conflicting emotions. Damn the woman. Damn her to hell for interrupting his new marriage and leaving him grappling with decisions and choices he had hoped were long resolved.

Morning light streamed through the windows, casting a warm glow over the elegantly set breakfast table. Alexander was greeted by the aroma of freshly brewed coffee and the bustling sounds of the household.

He found the sisters already gathered around the table, engaged in lively conversation. Mary recounted a tale from a book she'd read, gesturing animatedly as she narrated the protagonist's adventures. Olivia listened intently, occasionally interjecting with her own musings. Caroline was focused on her plate, seemingly lost in thought, though she occasionally nodded in agreement.

Eleanor sat at the head of the table, presiding over the morning meal with serene grace. She caught Alexander's eye, offered a warm smile, and welcomed him with a nod. He returned the gesture. Everything would be okay. He'd make sure of it.

He kissed the back of her hand before settling into the seat opposite her. A servant promptly poured him a cup of coffee before refilling Eleanor's cup with tea.

Caroline delicately sipped her tea before glancing at Olivia, a mischievous smile on her lips. "When do you plan to debut, Olivia?"

Olivia raised an eyebrow, slightly caught off guard. "Debut? I'm not sure that's in my plans for the immediate future."

Eleanor, ever the mediator, chimed in, "You should debut first, Olivia. It's tradition for the older sister to debut before her younger siblings, and you, my dear, are next in line."

Olivia shook her head. "I don't see the necessity. Besides, I have other interests I wish to pursue."

Caroline, ever the persistent one, leaned in with a playful grin. "Come on, Liv. It is about time you made your grand entrance. You will shine, I'm sure. And I cannot debut until you do."

Olivia fidgeted with her teacup, not entirely convinced. "I will think about it, but I am not making any promises."

Eleanor intervened gently. "Let's not pressure her, Caroline. Olivia will decide in her own time."

The conversation lingered, the sisters exchanging subtle glances, each with her own opinion on the matter. Olivia remained steadfast in her reluctance. For some unknown reason, she seemed quite unwilling to conform to the expectations of noble young women.

The room echoed with laughter, the sisters' bond evident in their easy interactions. Alexander found himself drawn into their world, one where familial ties were cherished, and each member was valued.

The gentle clinking of cutlery and the soft murmur of voices enveloped the room, weaving a comforting atmosphere. Despite finding himself surrounded by women, amid a realm of pure femininity unfamiliar to him, and surrounded by the poised formality of standing servants awaiting commands, the gathering exuded a familial ease. In the intimacy of their morning routine, Alexander discovered a profound sense of belonging, grounding him amidst the gentle chaos of the moment.

Throughout the meal, Eleanor seamlessly multitasked, offering thoughtful insights while attending to the needs of her sisters. She poured tea for Olivia, passed the butter to Caroline, and exchanged a knowing glance with Mary whenever the conversation turned amusingly lively.

As usual, Lady Beatrice made a spectacular entrance. Every gaze turned to watch her glide further into the breakfast room, already dressed in a deep sapphire gown that perfectly complemented her regal bearing. Her elegantly styled silver hair shimmered under the soft glow of chandeliers.

Every movement she made seemed choreographed, her steps purposeful, and her posture impeccably straight. Alexander was used to her, but he still found himself impressed.

"It would seem I overslept. I have missed the best part of breakfast." With a penetrating gaze that missed nothing, Lady Beatrice surveyed the room, her piercing blue eyes assessing each person present.

She took her seat and turned her attention to Olivia. "Now that your sister is married, we must turn our focus to you, don't you agree?"

She placed a napkin on her lap. "You are already eighteen, is that correct?"

Olivia, sitting nearby, glanced up, a frown etched on her face. "I am not in the mood for this. Excuse me."

"Well, I never!" Lady Beatrice exclaimed. "What's gotten into her?"

Eleanor leaned forward, her tone calm and resolute. "She needs some space, Lady Weston. We will discuss it later."

Beatrice huffed in frustration but nodded, no doubt realizing the need for a more delicate approach. With a resigned sigh, she agreed, "Very well, but her debut cannot be put off for too long. She is almost on the shelf already."

"Hardly that, Lady Beatrice." Eleanor remarked. "I will encourage her, of course, but she is only eighteen. There is plenty of time to find her a husband."

Alexander gently covered Eleanor's hand with his own. "Eleanor speaks wisely, Grandmother. Let us not burden the sisters with undue pressure, especially as they have only just emerged from mourning for their father."

A subtle heaviness settled over the atmosphere, and Alexander inwardly lamented broaching the topic of their father's passing.

Eleanor broke the silence that followed. "Was there anything of significance in your mail today, Alexander?"

His shoulders tightened. Had she recognized the handwriting? No. How could she? He set down his fork as he debated how much to disclose, if anything. "Just the usual affairs, nothing pressing." He aimed for a nonchalant tone to mask his unease.

As Eleanor's question and his rather stilted answer hung in the air, Alexander instinctively averted his gaze from her and focused intently on his plate. He felt her eyes fixed upon him, a gentle scrutiny that seemed to penetrate the surface of his composed façade. He hadn't read the letter yet, but he hardly needed to. The damned woman wanted money from him, no doubt in his mind. A pang of guilt pricked at him as he wrestled with the decision to withhold the truth from Eleanor.

He tried to eat as he normally would. With each bite, his mind teetered between revealing the source of the letter and maintaining the appearance of normalcy. Eleanor remained silent. The weight of unspoken words loomed heavily in the space between them, a silent barrier that tested his resolve. Despite the sisters' efforts to bury the disquiet, the discomfort lingered, a palpable presence during an otherwise ordinary morning meal.

He nearly choked on a piece of potato, his mind swirling with doubt. Could Eleanor see through his façade? No, he couldn't entertain such thoughts. He had to cling to hope that she remained oblivious to his inner turmoil. The delicate truths they had forged together last night now stood on the brink of collapse, all because of a letter he had neither expected nor wanted, from a woman he wanted nothing to do with.

And yet, a gnawing sensation in his gut whispered that she knew he was keeping something from him. And if she found out, he also knew her heart would break all over again, and this time, there would be no coming back from it.

Chapter Seventeen

Eleanor's fingers glided across the ivory keys of the grand pianoforte, weaving a melody that resonated throughout the opulent chamber. Once a source of solace, the music now felt hollow, unable to dispel the disquiet that had settled within her since yesterday.

Alexander had been distant of late, a subtle shift in his demeanor that Eleanor couldn't decipher. At first, she dismissed it as the combined weight of his responsibilities as Lord and his newly acquired responsibility as husband and guardian of her sisters and mother. But it went deeper, she was sure. She sensed an unspoken tension, an uncharted territory between them.

As she played, she darted her gaze towards the door, alternately dreading and anticipating Alexander's arrival, hoping for a shared moment to dissolve the veil of secrecy surrounding him. Yet, the door remained closed, his absence keenly felt.

The melody faltered, notes stumbling over one another as Eleanor's concentration waned. With a sigh that seemed to come from her very core, she stilled her fingers on the keys.

The unease that gnawed at her heart grew stronger, morphing into a persistent ache that felt almost like a living, breathing entity within her. It was as if a small creature had taken residence in her chest, its claws digging deeper with each passing moment of Alexander's absence. This creature, this unsettling presence, whispered doubts and fears into her mind, casting shadows where once there was only light.

With every beat of her heart, Eleanor felt its weight pressing down on her, a heaviness that threatened to suffocate her. It was a constant companion, a silent observer of her inner turmoil, and no matter how hard she attempted to ignore it, it refused to be ignored.

As she sat at the pianoforte, her fingers trembling ever so slightly, Eleanor couldn't shake the feeling of being watched. It was as if the creature within her had grown restless, its agitated energy palpable in the air around her.

And yet despite the unease that gripped her, Eleanor couldn't bring herself to confront the source of her fears. The thought of facing Alexander, of peeling back the layers of secrecy that surrounded him, filled her with a sense of dread. She was afraid of what she might find. Of the truths that lay hidden beneath the surface of their relationship.

So, she played on, her music a desperate plea for clarity amid chaos, her heart aching with the weight of the unknown. For now, all she could do was wait, hoping against hope that somehow, some way, the truth would reveal itself and bring an end to the unease that consumed her.

"Eleanor?"

The voice, startling in its suddenness, made her jump. She turned to see Alexander standing in the doorway, his expression inscrutable as he observed her.

"Alexander," she greeted him softly, a glimmer of hope sparking in her chest. "You're here."

He crossed the room in measured steps. "Indeed, I am."

His tone was crisp, his spine as stiff as one of his freshly starched shirts. Eleanor shifted on the bench, her fingers tracing the edge of a key absentmindedly. She drew on years of training to keep her tone neutral, gentle, and completely free of apprehension. "Is something amiss?"

He hesitated, a fleeting moment of indecision flashing across his features before he moved to stand behind her, his hand resting lightly on her shoulder. "No, of course not."

He was lying. She wasn't sure when she realized she knew him well enough to be able to tell, but there was no doubt in her mind.

Eleanor's heart plummeted, engulfed by a tidal wave of emotions that threatened to capsize her. She yearned to reach across the ever-expanding gulf between them that seemed to widen with each tick of the clock, but everything about his tone and posture erected an impregnable fortress around him.

"What did you need?" Her inquiry floated in the air, barely a murmur.

Alexander's hand tightened briefly on her shoulder before he withdrew it and stepped to face her, a pained expression flitting across his face. "I must go to London for a few days on urgent business. I leave on the morrow."

She lifted her gaze to meet his, her eyes pleading for understanding. But he remained closed off.

"Understood," she replied softly.

He let out a breath. Had she made him nervous? He gave a slight smile. "I plan to bring a doctor for your mother. I've found someone who might be able to help."

The words offered little solace to Eleanor. She returned her attention to the keys before her, the once familiar music now a haunting reminder of the rift between her and the man she called her husband. As her fingers resumed their dance on the pianoforte, her heart echoed the melody, yearning for a harmony that seemed elusive.

Eleanor paused, her fingers hovering over the keys as a sudden resolve took hold of her. She faced Alexander again, determination stiffening her spine.

She jutted her chin forward. "I'd like to travel with you to London."

Alexander's expression faltered, a conflicted shadow crossing his features. He opened his mouth as if to speak then closed it again, his gaze averted.

"Please, Alexander," Eleanor pressed, her voice tinged with urgency. "I feel as though something…"

No. She wouldn't speak all her concerns out loud. But she would let him know that she hadn't believed his lie. "If there's anything I can do to help, let me."

Alexander met her gaze, his eyes a stormy sea of emotions battling within. "Eleanor, it's not safe—"

"I don't care," she interrupted, her voice unwavering. "I will not be left behind while you face whatever is you are searching for. If the answer lies in London, then take me with you. I can help. I can at least be by your side, as your wife should be."

"The roads are worse than when we arrived. I expect the trip back to London will take longer and be a damn sight more uncomfortable."

"I am aware." Her eyes narrowed. Seven or eight hours in a carriage bumping over rutted roads might be less than ideal, but worth it to achieve her aim.

Alexander's shoulders slumped slightly, a silent surrender to Eleanor's unwavering determination. He sighed, a mixture of resignation and reluctance evident in his voice. "Very well. If it's what you wish, I'll arrange for us to depart for London together."

Though he relented, the lines etched on his brow betrayed his reluctance. Eleanor sensed the weight of his acquiescence, an acknowledgment that this journey held dangers from which he wished to shield her.

"Thank you." She gave him what she hoped was a bright smile. Somehow, she had to keep her unease hidden.

Alexander nodded, a faint hint of a weary smile gracing his lips. "Promise me, Eleanor, that you will exercise caution. Our marriage is still young, and the members of the ton have long memories and love nothing more than a scandal."

If there was anyone who understood the ton's hypersensitivity to the faintest hint of scandal, it was her. Her heart thrummed with a potent mix of anxiety and resolve. Opting against verbal sparring, she offered a nod of acquiescence and laced her voice with sincerity. "I promise."

Alexander left the room to attend to preparations for their journey. She had no doubt that whatever awaited them in London held the key to the mystery shrouding her husband, and she was determined to uncover the truth, no matter the cost.

Eleanor rose from the pianoforte with a determined grace and walked to her elegant bedchamber to pack.

As Alexander had requested, and with no objections from Eleanor, they shared the comfortable bed in his room every night, but this adjoining room made a perfect place for her to dress and undress, bathe, and for Lucy to attend to her hair.

Lucy, her maid and a gift from Lady Beatrice, trotted into the room moments later. Together, they selected garments suitable for her upcoming journey. She chose practical attire, yet among the dresses and cloaks, she tucked away a few items that whispered of her life before marriage—a cherished silk scarf, a locket holding a portrait of her parents. Was she clutching at them as if they could shield her from an uncertain future?

She was embarking on this journey with a purpose that transcended the mundane. A quiver started in her stomach and worked its way up until it lodged as a hard lump in her throat. Alexander had betrayed her once before, and it was difficult not to worry about what he was hiding this time. Hopefully, she could unravel the enigma surrounding him, or at least understand the depth of his secrecy and the shadows that haunted him.

The chamber echoed with the soft rustle of fabric as her maid wrapped each of her gowns in muslin and packed them in her traveling trunk.

Her bedroom door creaked open.

"May we come in?" Olivia didn't wait for an invitation.

With a regal bearing and a disapproving frown etched upon her features, she entered the room and stood before Eleanor. Caroline followed, a mischievous twinkle in her eye, while Mary trailed behind, her gaze dreamy and filled with curiosity.

Olivia glanced around the room, her disapproval deepening at the sight of the packed trunk. "Why is your maid packing for you? Where are you going? What's going on?"

Caroline joined Olivia and crossed her arms. "Are you off on a secret adventure without us, Ellie?"

Mary glanced between the trunk and Eleanor; her eyes wide. "Are we going somewhere exciting? Are you going without us?"

Eleanor rubbed at her temples, a knot tightening in her stomach. She didn't like the thought of lying to her sisters. Not even by omission. With a deep sigh she straightened her shoulders, she didn't like lying, so she wouldn't.

She faced the three younger women who gazed at her with varying degrees of concern. "Please don't worry about anything. I won't be leaving you for long. Alexander has business to attend to in London, and I will be accompanying him."

"But why London, of all places?" Olivia's disapproving gaze sharpened; her voice laced with concern. "There is nothing for you there except the memories of scandal and distorted gossip. I understand why you married him, I really do, but you are developing feelings. You must remember that the man is a cad. This marriage has been nothing but trouble. You should not be following him blindly."

Eleanor opened her mouth to respond, to perhaps defend Alexander. She wasn't sure, and Caroline interrupted before she could straighten out her thoughts.

Caroline smirked, unable to resist teasing in the middle of a standoff between her two older sisters. "Perhaps Ellie is finally taking charge. Are you really mooning after him, or are you planning to uncover some scandalous secrets to hold over him?"

Eleanor stiffened. Caroline's words struck to her core.

Mary's eyes widened with excitement. "Is it a secret mission, like those in the novels I read? Will there be scandals and secrets, hidden mysteries and daring adventures?"

Eleanor traversed the breadth of the room and returned, her restless pacing betraying the turmoil within, yet she found herself powerless to halt her ceaseless movement. "I don't know what awaits us in London." She rotated her neck to try to alleviate the tension that had stealthily claimed her. When had her shoulders become so burdened? Her sisters observed in silent anticipation, their eyes wide with unspoken questions.

Eleanor didn't want to frighten them or say something she didn't know the answer to, but she refused to lie. "There are things Alexander hasn't told me, and I need to find out what he is hiding."

Olivia stepped closer and reached towards her. "Eleanor, you cannot go chasing after shadows. Please consider your safety and reputation. This marriage has barely saved both your reputation and the family honor. Won't returning to London so quickly remind the gossips of what happened not that long ago?"

Eleanor lifted her brow. "Or perhaps the ton will observe us together and remark upon how the stories spread by Lady Beatrice must be true, and I am not a woman lacking virtue after all."

Caroline placed a hand on Olivia's shoulder. "Livy, let Ellie have her adventure. Who knows what secrets she might uncover?"

Mary clasped her hands together, a sparkle in her eyes. "I think it's terribly exciting and romantic. I'm sure Eleanor will present a vision of happily married bliss to the *ton*. But do be careful, my darling, and tell us everything when you return."

Their varied reactions mirrored Eleanor's own conflicting emotions. She offered them a tentative smile, grateful for their concern and support. Even though Olivia tended to cover her concern with anger, Eleanor knew it came from a place of love.

A sense of responsibility toward the girls weighed heavily upon her. She'd always taken a large role in their care, especially in the last six months. This would be the first time they were apart.

She reached out to embrace all three in a big hug. "While I'm away, I expect everyone to continue your studies diligently. Olivia, Caroline, Mary, you must promise me that. And remember that Lady Beatrice is here and has taken you under her wing."

Olivia's disapproval softened into concern as she glanced at her younger sisters, but she nodded her agreement. "We will, Eleanor. But are you sure you must go?"

Eleanor held Olivia's gaze, a silent understanding passing between them. "Yes, I must. And I need you to watch over them for me, Olivia."

Olivia crossed her arms and harrumphed. "If you stayed, you could watch us yourself. Must you really leave?"

"There are things I need to understand." Eleanor took Olivia's hands in her own. How could she tell them she wanted the married bliss, that she didn't give a damn what the ton thought of her if her sisters received the best debut possible, and that she so badly wanted to love her husband it hurt, but she couldn't until she learned the truth? Instead, she steeled herself. "I have to do this."

Olivia's features softened as she recognized the determination in Eleanor's voice. After a moment's pause, she nodded again, though with obvious reluctance.

Eleanor pulled Olivia into an embrace, a mixture of gratitude and regret coursing through her. "Thank you, Olivia," she murmured. "I trust you to look after them in my absence."

Olivia returned the hug, her voice barely above a whisper. "I hope you find what you're looking for, Eleanor."

As she completed her preparations for the trip, a knot formed in her chest, the realization of the ramifications of the journey ahead settling heavily upon her. But she would carry forward Olivia's hope and add her own. She gazed out the window to the blue sky beyond and issued a silent prayer. *Please let me find what I'm looking for.*

Chapter Eighteen

Alexander tapped on the adjoining door and entered Eleanor's bedchamber. Lucy had finished wrapping Eleanor's dresses in muslin and was laying Eleanor's toiletries on the bed, ready for packing in her dressing case. He glanced at hair whitener, a pot of pink rouge, scented waters, soap, several linen handkerchiefs with a lace trim, a sewing kit and her writing box.

Bur his gaze lingered on his Eleanor, the woman whose resilience and unwavering spirit both captivated and worried him. He admired her strength, her insistence on uncovering the truths that had remained veiled since their union, yet he couldn't shake the gnawing fear that this pursuit would lead to peril.

The conflicting storm of emotions in his mind seemed to be a good match for the bustle in the room.

"Come, Lady Weston." He held out his hand for her to take. "Let us get some sleep. We must rise early."

"Sleep, Lord Weston?" She raised her eyebrows, a sparkle of mischief in her gaze. But she stepped to him and took his hand.

"A little sleep, at least. I dare say we can always nod off in the carriage tomorrow."

She laughed, but he noted the tension in her bearing, the slight tremor in her voice. "I doubt there will be much nodding off with the rutted roads."

The carriage rattled along winding roads, every so often lurching to one side or the other as one of the wheels caught in a rut.

Eleanor sat beside him, her posture poised, yet he detected the subtle tension in her demeanor. His worry for her safety and his secrets intensified with every passing mile. He stole glances at her, her profile etched against the backdrop of the passing countryside, her thoughts veiled behind her composure. Alexander yearned to ease her fears, to confide in her, yet the shadows of his own past loomed large, imprisoning him in silence.

As London's distant skyline came into view, Alexander's heart clenched. He had no doubt at all that nothing good would come from another meeting with Abigail. He stole a glance at Eleanor, the resolute set of her jaw betraying her determination. She was adamant in her pursuit of truth, a pursuit that filled him with both admiration and dread.

Alexander grappled with the weight of secrets he dared not share, and the overwhelming need to protect the woman by his side. He wanted to protect her from himself almost as much as he wanted to protect her from the scorn of the *ton*.

The carriage came to a halt before his elegant townhouse. Eleanor's gaze swept over the grand and symmetrical façade, her expression a mix of awe and curiosity. The wrought iron gates opened, granting entry to the stately home that held within its walls centuries of family history and prestige.

He tried to see the stone frontage with tall sash windows evenly spaced across multiple floors through her eyes but failed. He'd known this home all his life. She took his arm, and he led her to a prominent doorcase atop imposing steps. Iron railings enclosed a small forecourt, adding to the dignified appearance.

His butler welcomed them inside, and Alexander guided Eleanor through the ornate foyer. He noted her admiring glances at the portraits lining the walls, each a testament to the lineage he was obligated to uphold. His heart swelled with conflicting emotions—pride in his heritage intertwined with the weight of responsibility that came with it.

He kissed her hand and led her past the grand staircase to the drawing room. Like the entire ground floor, it had recently been redecorated in the finest craftsmanship money could buy. Pastel green silk wallpaper adorned the walls. Artwork, including portraits of ancestors and landscapes, hung in gilded frames alongside mirrors with ornate carvings, enhancing the light and space. All the furniture was of the highest quality and richly upholstered in sumptuous velvet. He was proud of his home, but if Eleanor wanted to redecorate, he'd have everything ripped out immediately.

In the drawing room, he struggled to mask his regret. "I must attend to urgent matters, my dear. Business calls, but I will return in time for dinner."

Eleanor nodded gracefully, a veil of politeness masking any disappointment she might have felt. "Of course, Alexander. It has been a tiring journey. I will change and acquaint myself with our London home."

Our London home. He'd wanted to share this home with her for so long, his breath hitched. He couldn't lose her. He wouldn't.

He pressed a gentle kiss to her forehead, a silent promise of his imminent return. Only the prominent weight of obligation could have pulled him away from Eleanor's side. As he stepped back out to his waiting phaeton, his thoughts lingered on her, uneasy flickers of worry clouding his mind.

Amidst the lively chaos of the city, Alexander's mind churned. He'd taken the reins himself and driven with a restless energy. The designated meeting place was in Southwark, and he'd visited the address only once before. Somehow, he remembered the way without even thinking about it. He headed southeast on Pall Mall, passed by St. James's Place, and continued towards Trafalgar Square. He manoeuvred around people and too many other carriages past Somerset House and a bustling area filled with shops, theatres, and coffee houses. Past St. Paul's Cathedral, he almost lost control going down Ludgate Hill, but thankfully, he'd kept hold of the reins and drove towards the river Thames. Blackfriars

Bridge was an obstacle course as usual, but once across, he sprinted into the borough of Southwark.

He pulled the carriage to a halt in front of a modest, weather-worn house nestled within a working-class neighborhood, a stark contrast to the opulence Alexander was accustomed to. The paint on the house was faded, some glass had been replaced with cardboard, and slate tiles on the steeply pitched roof showed obvious signs of poor repairs.

He didn't recall the place being this run down. Then again, it had been a while since he'd last visited.

Alexander alighted from the carriage, the curious gazes from passersby a weight on his shoulders. Pedestrians, their attire suggesting lives steeped in toil and struggle, eyed the luxurious carriage with suspicion. The contrast between the opulent vehicle and the humble surroundings was stark, drawing unwelcome attention that made Alexander uneasy.

He handed the reins to his man, Johnson, with a nod. He was a good man, an ex-soldier, and perfect to guard his favorite vehicle.

Gathering his resolve, Alexander straightened his coat. He cast a fleeting glance at his surroundings, hoping this would indeed be the final visit to this unassuming house.

With a quick glance towards those who continued to eye the carriage suspiciously, Alexander approached the humble house, the anticipation of concluding this clandestine chapter of his life lending an urgency to his steps.

He rapped his knuckles against the weathered door, the sound echoing in the quiet street. Moments later, it creaked open, revealing Abigail. A woman of Eleanor's age, long ago one of Eleanor's best friends. That wasn't the case anymore.

Abigail gave him a sardonic smirk. "I knew you'd come."

The edge of smugness in her tone irked Alexander. He entered, and the familiar yet distant atmosphere within the small house settled uneasily around him. His nostrils flared with displeasure, but he cared little that his behavior and tone betrayed his displeasure at being in her presence. "Abigail, this will be the last time I visit you here. Or anywhere else."

Abigail, unfazed by his declaration, closed the door behind him with a resolute click. "Is that so?" she countered, a hint of challenge in her tone. "Then perhaps I should tell your new bride everything."

Alexander's expression hardened, a surge of frustration mingling with the anxiety that churned within him. "You wouldn't dare." His lips pinched and his hands gripped behind his back gave away his frustration.

The tension in the air crackled as Alexander and Abigail stood facing each other, each holding the weight of unspoken truths. The threat of unraveling the carefully constructed mask that shielded Eleanor from the secrets of the past hung ominously between them.

With a steely resolve, Alexander squared his shoulders, his voice firm and unwavering. "I want no more correspondence. No more contact. Not with me, not with my family. Our arrangement is finished."

Abigail regarded him with a cool detachment, her gaze betraying a hint of defiance. "I suppose we'll see." Her tone carried an enigmatic edge that left Alexander uneasy.

Whether he wanted to admit it or not, Abigail had all the power here. If he wanted to move on with his life, he had no choice but to do exactly as she said. Because if Eleanor ever found out about this, any chance of happiness he could have with her would be ruined forever.

Chapter Nineteen

Despite attempts to mask her apprehension, a gnawing sense of unease clawed at Eleanor's chest. She stood in the vast drawing room, the grandeur of the house that had once seemed impressive now felt cavernous and foreboding in its emptiness.

Determination and dread swirled within her, but Eleanor decided to explore the unfamiliar ground floor, a feeble attempt to distract herself from the haunting uncertainties that lingered in her mind. She traversed through the elegantly adorned corridors, her steps echoing against the polished floors. How she wished her sisters were here with her, or Alexander. She missed him already, and never felt so alone. Each corner of the opulent house seemed to emanate a cold air of secrecy that left her feeling isolated.

"Can I help you, Lady Weston?"

Startled, Eleanor let out a screech.

"Do forgive me, my lady. I did not mean to startle you."

It took a moment, but then Eleanor recognized the butler who'd let them into Alexander's home.

Her pulse still raced, but she calmed her breathing enough to speak. "I'm afraid I was gathering wool. I need no help, thank you, I am merely exploring."

"Of course." He gave her a small bow. "Do let me know if you need anything at all." He pointed to one of the bellpulls that she'd seen prominently placed in each room and at several points along the hallways. It was good to know she could gain attention so quickly.

Wandering through the lavish rooms, Eleanor was drawn to the decor's intricate details, the artistry of the furnishings, and the delicate wall embellishments. But each exquisite painting and ornate furniture piece just seemed to emphasise her isolation.

Her steps faltered before a closed door. The memory of the ball night was vivid in her mind. Too vivid. With a shaky breath, she opened it to reveal a dimly lit study, a quiet space lined with bookshelves, and a desk cluttered with papers. Yet, her concern was elsewhere, focused on her husband's mysterious absence and secretive meetings, stirring a tempest of worry within her.

As she retraced her steps, the grandeur of the house failed to comfort her. The luxury felt hollow against haunting uncertainties surrounding her husband's secrets. The silence of the empty house echoed her fears, deepening her sense of dread.

Lost in thoughts regarding her husband's enigmatic actions, she was startled by a woman rounding the corner. The woman, with a look of concern, introduced herself as Mrs. Gilbert, the housekeeper, and apologized for startling her. "Apologies, Lady Weston. I've been searching everywhere for you," Mrs. Gilbert said, her soothing hazel eyes filled with worry and surprise. "It's a pleasure to meet you."

Mrs. Gilbert was a woman of seasoned grace, her years etched upon a countenance weathered by time but softened by a gentle warmth that emanated from her kind, hazel eyes. Her silver-streaked hair was neatly coiled into a bun, wisps escaping to frame a face adorned with soft lines that spoke of a lifetime of wisdom and care. Despite the simplicity of her attire—a modest dress adorned with a crisp apron—there was an air of dignity about her, an unspoken authority that commanded respect.

Her weathered hands, calloused from years of meticulous labor, now held a duster. The faint scent of lavender wafted around her, a familiar fragrance that carried with it a sense of comfort and familiarity.

Mrs. Gilbert's warm smile was tinged with an apologetic air as she stood before Eleanor. "Begging your pardon, Lady Weston. I've been searching high and low for you. I must admit, I wasn't expecting Lord Weston to return here so soon after you were wed."

Eleanor's brow furrowed slightly, a silent acknowledgment of Mrs. Gilbert's unexpected urgency. "Is something the matter, Mrs. Gilbert?"

Mrs. Gilbert's eyes widened slightly, a fleeting expression of regret crossing her face. "I'm sorry we are not quite ready for you, my lady. Like I said, I wasn't expecting Lord Weston to arrive, especially not with yourself accompanying him. I give you my word that the whole place will be in perfect order before we retire this evening."

Eleanor gave the other woman a slight smile and a nod. If Alexander had surprised them with their visit, it was no wonder even the housekeeper busied herself with cleaning tasks.

But as Eleanor processed Mrs. Gilbert's words, her mind grappled with the implications of the housekeeper's unexpected flurry of activity. As she offered the older woman a reassuring smile, Eleanor couldn't shake the foreboding sense that whatever Alexander was up to, no one else, not even his staff, knew about it.

"Thank you, Mrs. Gilbert. I'll continue my tour of the house for now, but please have dinner prepared promptly at 8pm in the dining room. I am expecting Alexander to return before then."

At least, she hoped so.

Mrs. Gilbert offered a quick, respectful bow before excusing herself, leaving Eleanor to traverse the grand halls once more. As the housekeeper disappeared around a corner, Eleanor's resolve solidified. She needed answers. She needed the clarity that had so far eluded her amidst the whirlwind of uncertainty surrounding Alexander's clandestine activities.

With determined steps, Eleanor veered toward Alexander's study, her heart pounding. Despite the trepidation that clawed at her chest, she pressed forward, her hand reaching for the doorknob.

Entering the dimly lit study, Eleanor was again greeted by the smell of leather-bound books and a hint of sandalwood, stirring a familiar comfort against the painful tension in her chest and shoulders. Her gaze swept over the meticulously arranged shelves and came to rest on the imposing desk cluttered with papers and reports, as if he'd been called away from the room before he could stack and tidy everything.

Everything in the room screamed Alexander's name. He'd obviously spent some time in this space, managing his affairs. Each book, every piece of art on the wall, the writing implements, it all seemed to capture a part of Alexander's mysterious life, inviting her curiosity.

Eleanor moved towards the desk, her touch light on its surface as she examined the documents. Was she behaving like a common busybody? The letters and ledgers whispered secrets of Alexander's intricate affairs, pulling her between the need for understanding and the guilt of prying.

But she was driven by a need to uncover the truth, so she stiffened her spine and delved into the paperwork.

She carefully examined the documents, hoping to uncover evidence of the hidden activities haunting her thoughts. Yet, as she moved through the routine correspondence and business notes, disappointment crept in. Apart from the papers on the desk, the orderliness of Alexander's study seemed to mock her search for answers, suggesting her efforts might be fruitless.

"Come on," she muttered. "I know something must be here."

As her hope dwindled, Eleanor's gaze fell upon the desk drawers. With a moment's hesitation, she pulled at the ornate handle, the drawer gliding open with a whisper. Among the neatly arranged stationery and personal effects, a crumpled letter caught her eye. It seemed out of place, an anomaly amidst the orderly arrangement of Alexander's possessions.

Her heart pounded against her ribcage as she gingerly plucked the wrinkled parchment from its hiding place. The paper felt brittle and worn beneath her trembling fingers as she smoothed it out with painstaking care. It was the correspondence he'd received at the estate. He'd brought it with him to London, perhaps mangled it in anger, but then stuffed it in this drawer.

Her breath hitched as the words upon it came into focus, the ink smudged as if the writer was too eager to wait for it to dry before folding the note.

With every unfolding crease, Eleanor's heart raced faster, her pulse pounding in her ears as she scanned the contents of the letter. Her eyes widened in disbelief as she pieced together the cryptic message written upon it, the words sending a chill down her spine.

My dearest Alexander,

Congratulations on the nuptials. I must admit, I never thought Eleanor would agree to marry you after everything that happened between you. Between us. Nevertheless, I trust your judgment and wish you both happiness in your union.

I find myself in need of your presence immediately. Urgent matters require your attention. Please come to London as soon as you can so that we can discuss these pressing issues in person.

Yours,

A

The weight of the letter's contents crashed upon Eleanor with an overwhelming force, her chest tightening as if the air itself had turned heavy and suffocating. The recognition of the familiar handwriting, the implications of the words, were a visceral blow that stole her breath. Panic surged within her, rendering each inhalation a laborious struggle.

Tears welled in her eyes, blurring the damning words on the parchment. A surge of emotions, a whirlwind of betrayal, confusion, and heartache, surged within her. It was the worst revelation, a damning confirmation of doubts that had previously lingered as whispers at the edges of her consciousness.

Eleanor's legs gave way beneath her, the weight of the truth proving too much to bear. She fell to her knees, the air thinning around her as sobs wracked her body.

Nausea churned within her, a tumultuous storm of emotions tearing through her being. She stumbled towards the waste bin, her movements clumsy and erratic, unable to contain the overwhelming rush of emotions. Her body revolted. and with a gut-wrenching heave, she emptied the contents of her stomach into the receptacle.

Barely able to catch her breath, tears streamed down her cheeks, mingling with the harsh reality that unfolded before her. It was a pain that cut deep, a betrayal that shattered the fragile trust she'd placed in her husband.

As Eleanor trembled, her entire being consumed by a whirlwind of emotions, Mrs. Gilbert rushed into the study. She let out a gasp and hurried to Eleanor's side, concern etched into the lines of her face.

"Lady Weston, dear me. What's happened? Are you unwell?" the servant's voice quivered with worry as she gently lifted Eleanor, offering her support and steadying her trembling form.

Eleanor clutched the letter tightly against her chest, her fingers curled around the parchment as if it were the only lifeline in the tempest that engulfed her. She couldn't bring herself to let go, not that she would forget the words or stop thinking about the voice speaking them.

"I'll take you to your room, my lady," Mrs. Gilbert said softly, guiding Eleanor with a comforting arm around her, leading her away from the study's suffocating atmosphere.

She leaned on the housekeeper for support, her body trembling and mind clouded by the shock of what she had discovered. Tears continued to streak down her cheeks, her emotions in tumultuous disarray.

Mrs. Gilbert guided her through the opulent corridors, her steps measured and gentle. As they reached Eleanor's room, the older woman helped her settle onto the edge of the bed, concern etched into every line on her face.

"My dear, can I do anything for you? Shall I fetch some tea? Or perhaps something to soothe your nerves?" Mrs. Gilbert's voice held an undercurrent of genuine care as she hovered nearby, ready to offer any comfort Eleanor might seek.

But Eleanor remained silent, her gaze fixed on the letter clutched tightly in her trembling hands. It was a damning testament to the fracture in her newfound happiness, an unwelcome truth that shattered the illusion of her marriage.

Chapter Twenty

Even as Alexander stepped through the threshold of his townhouse, the weight of the encounter with Abigail still clung to him like an unwelcome shadow. His features, typically composed, were etched with a furrowed brow, pinched lips and clenched jaw. A sense of frustration like he'd never felt before simmered within.

His discussion with Abigail lingered, leaving a bitter taste in his mouth as he ascended the stairs, his footsteps echoing in the silence. He yearned for the warmth of home, a respite from the tumultuous affairs that plagued his thoughts. He wanted to leave London immediately and race away with his tail between his legs. But not with Eleanor here.

Not yet.

Dragging her back so quickly would only arouse her suspicion further.

Arriving at the dining room, his mood darkened upon noticing Eleanor's absence. The table, adorned with fine linens and gleaming silverware, stood empty, devoid of the lively presence that typically graced their dinners. A pang of concern shot through him, an unexpected worry gnawing at his gut as he scanned the room, searching for any sign of her.

Anxiety joined the frustration clawing at Alexander's composure, his gaze darting to the ornate clock that ticked away the moments. Eleanor was always punctual. Her absence was now cause for concern. He fought the impulse to shout out her name, his mind clouded due to the day's events and the secrets he guarded.

A sense of foreboding crept over him, an unsettling feeling that something was amiss, that the delicate balance of their union was teetering on the edge. He attempted to push aside the lingering disquiet, opting instead to take his seat at the head of the table, albeit with a sense of restlessness that refused to be quelled.

Minutes passed, each ticking second heightening his unease. The absence of Eleanor's presence was a haunting void.

As the hands of the clock continued their relentless march, Alexander's concern deepened into a knot of worry. His impatience grew, and he couldn't shake the unease that gripped him.

He rose from his seat. "Mrs. Gilbert!" he shouted louder than he intended. Too late to change that now.

Moments later, the door swung open, and the servant hurried in and sketched a quick curtsy. "Forgive me, my lord. We are at sixes and sevens getting everything ready for you and her ladyship—"

"Where is Lady Weston?" His worry was evident in the furrow of his brow and the tension in his posture, but he could do nothing to stop his concern from showing.

"Lady Weston was ill earlier, sir. She's been in her room since. I've tried to coax her into eating, but she won't heed my words." Mrs. Gilbert's concern shone in her eyes. "She won't even take a cup of tea, sir."

Without a word, Alexander strode purposefully towards the door, a sense of urgency propelling him forward.

"Have you sent for the doctor?" Alexander gestured for the housekeeper to follow him to Eleanor's room.

"She straight up refused to see a doctor, sir. When I mentioned it for the third time, she shouted at me to leave her alone." Mrs. Gilbert sniffed.

Damnation, what was going on? Eleanor rarely lost her temper, and he'd never known her to shout at the staff. Alexander started taking the stairs two at a time, leaving the older woman well behind.

The silence that greeted him outside Eleanor's door felt deafening, amplifying his worry. He took a steadying breath, steeling himself for what he might find beyond the threshold. The door opened into darkness, not even a candle easing the gloom.

Alexander nodded once to dismiss Mrs. Gilbert. As the door closed behind her, he turned towards Eleanor, who sat perched upon the window seat, her silhouette framed against the dimming light filtering through the glass from the streetlight outside.

His heart constricted at the sight of her, her posture radiating a fragile vulnerability that tugged at his emotions. He lit one of the candles by the door. The first thing he noticed was a piece of paper lying at her feet.

She knew.

Somehow, she'd found the letter from Abigail.

He couldn't even fathom her snooping. But it didn't matter. The only thing that mattered was that she knew about Abigail contacting him.

Approaching her with cautious steps, Alexander's gaze lingered on Eleanor's profile, her gaze fixed upon the outside world. A world he feared might have crumbled within her. The air in the room felt charged, pregnant with unspoken words and the weight of shared revelations.

"Eleanor." His voice was soft, a hesitant attempt to breach the tense silence that enveloped them. He wanted to comfort her, to erase the pain etched on her features. He longed to ease her distress, to explain the tangled web of his past.

The gravity of his deception, the betrayals woven into the fabric of their union, were now laid bare before her.

She didn't react to him at all. Did he draw closer, try to calm her, blurt out the awful truth?

The silence rang louder with every passing heartbeat. Alexander's chest tightened, grappling with the emotions that surged within him. He swallowed several times. He had to try, had to somehow find the right words. But Eleanor spoke first.

"I need to understand, Alexander." Eleanor's voice wavered; her gaze locked onto his with an intensity that pierced through his defenses.

"Why did you leave me? Why go back to her? Why marry me if you still see Abigail?"

Eleanor's voice pierced the air around her, each word resonating with an arrow of pain that clawed at Alexander's chest and ripped his core into shreds. Her questions hung in the air, laden with the weight of betrayal and shattered trust, echoing the tumult that raged within him.

The words struck Alexander like a blow. He struggled to find the right words to convey the depth of his feelings, the tangled web of regrets that bound him.

"Eleanor, you have to believe me," Alexander found himself pleading. Now that he had found Eleanor again, he would not lose her. He couldn't bear it. "I love you. I have always loved you. Can't you see that?"

Eleanor's eyes reflected the hurt that festered beneath the surface. She demanded truth amidst the veil of deception that had clouded their union, leaving Alexander acutely aware of the chasm that separated them.

"How am I supposed to believe you?" Her voice trembled; her anguish palpable. "How can I possibly trust you when you lie to me? When you sneak off without a word..."

The weight of her accusation bore down on him, the ache in her words tearing a hole in his chest, a tangible reminder of the wounds he'd inflicted. Alexander's heart clenched, torn between the love he held for Eleanor and the shards of his past that threatened to unravel the fragile harmony between them.

"Eleanor, I never meant to hurt you." Alexander's voice cracked with emotion; his own turmoil laid bare. "I've made mistakes, but my love for you is true. I married you because you are everything to me. You must understand. Please."

His plea hung in the air.

He'd never felt so vulnerable. He could only hope that she could see in his expression a silent plea for her forgiveness, for the opportunity to bridge the chasm that threatened to consume their love.

"Help me understand, Alexander. Do you love her?"

His immediate response was a fervent denial, the words rushed yet earnest. "No, Eleanor, I do not and never have. I only see her because I must. It has nothing to do with love. It is... it's a complicated situation."

The weight of her gaze bore down upon him, her eyes probing for a clarity he struggled to provide. Alexander felt the weight of the unspoken truth pressing against his lips, the desire to confess everything conflicting with the fear of shattering the fragile trust Eleanor had in him.

"You can't expect me to accept your words, pretty though they are," she said. "You must explain. I do not care if it is complicated. Tell me, I beg you. Help me understand."

Alexander's lips parted, a silent struggle raging within him. He longed to share the tangled web of his past, to untangle the knots of deceit and reveal the raw truth that plagued his conscience. Yet the words remained trapped, ensnared by his own hesitations and the fear of the irreparable damage they might cause.

Time seemed to stretch into an agonizing eternity. Eleanor's unwavering gaze demanded transparency; a demand Alexander felt he couldn't fulfill despite his yearning to ease her pain.

"I... I cannot tell you," Alexander finally admitted, his voice barely above a whisper as he averted his gaze, unable to meet the intensity of Eleanor's eyes. His admission weighed on his shoulders, a confession of his own limitations and the barriers he couldn't overcome.

A wave of frustration washed over him. He longed to mend the wounds that festered, yet the tangled threads of his past held him captive in a web of secrecy and regret.

In the moment that followed, a palpable tension lingered, a barrier that threatened to irreversibly alter the course of their relationship.

"Cannot or will not, Alexander?" Eleanor stiffened, her voice no longer wavering.

He hesitated, pangs of regret and sorrow stabbing into his soul. "I want to, Eleanor, but I cannot."

How could he tell her the truth without shattering everything she'd ever believed about her life and love?

Her gaze hardened, a steely resolve settling within her. "If you cannot trust me, then there is no point in continuing this conversation. Please leave."

Alexander wanted to plead his case, beg her to forget this whole episode. He'd give Abigail whatever she wanted to leave them alone. But Eleanor's expression was so guarded, her posture so closed off, now was not the time, and he needed to guard his own mouth before he blurted out everything he'd tried to keep from her.

"You need to eat." If he couldn't ease her worries yet, perhaps he could at least show her he cared in other ways.

"You have no right to dictate what I do anymore." She shook her head, her voice laced with a bitter edge. Eleanor's unwavering gaze held his own. "As I feared, this marriage is nothing but a sham."

The weight of her words weighed on Alexander.

He almost fell to his knees. The chasm between them seemed insurmountable, their once-strong connection now fractured beyond repair. His heart clenched at the realization that his actions had irreparably damaged the foundation of their relationship.

"I knew I should not have married you," she muttered, more to herself than to him. "I should have faced a ruined reputation rather than tie myself to a rogue who will never change."

His heart ached at her words; the weight of his own failures heavy upon his shoulders. He stood there, a sense of helplessness washing over him. He loved her. How could he assure her of just how much he loved her? No point in blaming Abigail, though he wanted to. His own actions had caused this breach between them.

Chapter Twenty-One

The following day, they journeyed back home to the estate in Buckinghamshire.

The entire arduous journey was marked by palpable tension and a silence so uncomfortable Eleanor wasn't sure how she was still able to breathe in the suffocating atmosphere.

Each passing mile seemed to magnify the rift that had formed between them and unravel their fractured relationship even further.

Any necessary conversation was stilted and strained. Words, when exchanged, were hollow and lacked the warmth that once characterized their interactions.

Upon returning home, Eleanor began moving her things back into her own room, making a point to lock the door that connected hers to Alexander's. It was not just a rearrangement of space, but like the final note in the symphony of their crumbling relationship.

She sent her maid away. She needed to move, to do something. Anything.

As she placed her belongings away, the quiet of the room seemed to echo the tension between Alexander and her, but she would not let herself cry. No, this was not the time for tears.

A gentle tap sounded at her door. "May I come in, Eleanor?"

Alexander sounded as lost as she felt. But damnation, she did not want to see him now. Why hadn't she locked the main door to her room when she'd nudged her maid out? She raced to the door to lock it, but Alexander beat her to it and entered the space.

His presence was a question hanging in the air, unanswered.

"Eleanor, there is no need for rashness. Please don't rush into any decisions. Let's talk."

His tone was low, choked with emotion. Pleading, almost. She had to steel her heart to stop herself from reaching out to him.

Eleanor turned her back to him and continued putting her things way in her dresser. "What is there to discuss if you will not tell me the truth?"

Alexander didn't move or speak. All Eleanor could hear was his fractured breathing before his admission came softly, "I cannot explain everything."

With a shaky breath, Eleanor spun to face him. "It is not about being rash, Alexander. It's about self-respect, something you've left me little of."

The room was charged with the tension of their broken connection.

Eleanor hung on to her pride and determination, a shield against the hurt that Alexander's betrayal had caused. The pain visible on his face mirrored the ache in her own heart, a silent testament to the depth of their shared turmoil.

Resuming her task, Eleanor's actions spoke of her need to protect herself, to assert some control over the wreckage of their union. The silent room became a witness to them, a stark reminder that some distances can't be bridged, some words couldn't mend what has been broken.

Alexander left without another word shortly after. Eleanor stood in the wake of his departure, grappling with the feelings that threatened to engulf her. It took every ounce of her strength to resist the impulse to chase after him.

Her limbs tingled with fatigue. Her breaths came too shallow. The grating ache in her heart felt as real as any other pain she had ever felt.

The door creaked open, and her sisters filed into the room, their concerned gazes fixed upon her.

"What happened, Eleanor?" Olivia's voice held a tone of gentle concern, but her gaze probed for answers. "You have only been gone for one day_"

"And Alexander looked like he wanted to throw up." Caroline paced to Eleanor and stroked her arm. "So do you, dearest. You are so pale. What has happened? What can we do?"

Eleanor tried to stand tall, but she wasn't sure that her legs could hold her up, so she slumped onto the edge of her bed instead. She gave her sisters a strained smile, a feeble attempt to mask the tumultuous storm raging within her. "It's nothing, just a misunderstanding. I would rather not talk about it right now."

"Is it Alexander? Has he hurt you?" Mary stood next to Caroline, her small hand a gentle weight on Eleanor's shoulder.

Her sisters' concern—their love—almost undid her.

Eleanor closed her eyes as she rubbed at her temples. "Please, dear sisters, do not pry. I am not ready to talk about it yet."

Eleanor's heart ached with the weight of her emotions, but she found a semblance of solace in the unspoken understanding between her and her sisters—a shared bond that weathered the storm of uncertainties and offered her a fragment of comfort.

"We will leave you be, for now." Olivia kissed her cheek. "But know that we are here whenever you are comfortable to share your distress. In the meantime, I intend to punch Lord Weston in the mouth."

"I will kick him where it hurts. Cook showed me how!" Mary clapped her hands, as if eager for the opportunity.

"Girls, please," she gasped until she saw the grins on their faces. She gave a small smile of her own. "I am not ready for teasing, but will be soon, I promise."

Her sisters left her in peace. Eleanor lingered in the quiet confines of her room, the recent tumult pressed heavily upon her, an unyielding weight on her soul. Time seemed only to magnify her sorrow, each moment stretching longer than the last, deepening her sense of loss.

It was grief not just for what had been, but also for dreams left unfulfilled. The love she had imagined with Alexander now a poignant echo of what might have been.

Days melded into one another, their passage marked only by the solitude that filled Eleanor's room, a silent testament to her deepening despair. In this quiet refuge, she wrestled with lingering questions and the sharp sting of broken promises, seeking a comfort that remained just out of reach.

Amidst the ache, Eleanor found herself in a paradoxical haven, her loneliness a bitter shield against the storm of emotions threatening to overwhelm her. Alexander's absence was a constant echo of their severed ties, his silence a heavy weight that spoke volumes of the growing divide between them.

She longed for resolution, for a gesture that might begin to mend the ruptured trust and offer a glimmer of hope amidst the wreckage of their union. Yet, the continuing silence from Alexander only served to widen the gap, leaving her longing for a resolution that seemed increasingly elusive, and cast a shadow of desolation over her already heavy heart.

Her silent room mirrored the hollow ache within her, a tangible reflection of her quest for answers and the harsh bite of truths left unsaid. Her heart yearned for closure, for an explanation that might bring solace to the shattered remnants of her fractured love.

But as days blurred into a seamless tapestry of melancholy, the absence of any movement towards reconciliation cemented the painful realization that the hope she had harbored for their future together was slipping away, lost amidst the secrets and silence that had irrevocably torn them apart.

Eleanor's fingers pressed against the ivory keys of the pianoforte, coaxing out a haunting melody. As the melancholy notes filled the room, an unexpected knock at the door shattered the fragile sanctuary she had built.

Her heart skipped a beat as she turned toward the entrance, her breath catching in her throat at the sight of Abigail standing in the doorway. Fury surged within Eleanor like a tempest.

She didn't even wait for the butler to announce the guest. She pushed him aside to reach her.

"What are you doing here?" Eleanor's voice quivered with indignation; her tone laced with an icy edge that mirrored the storm brewing within her.

Abigail, undeterred by the palpable tension, offered a nonchalant smile. "I need to see Alexander. It is important.

She glanced around with an air of causal indifference, as if hoping to find him secreted away in her music room.

"How dare you come here, to my home." Eleanor's voice rose, her anger barely contained. "You're the reason my life is in turmoil, and now you have the audacity to show up at here?"

Abigail's composure faltered momentarily, a fleeting hint of unease and guilt crossing her features before she composed herself. "I need to see Alexander. It really is an urgent matter," she repeated, attempting to maintain her cool demeanor.

Eleanor stood her ground, her eyes ablaze. "You have no right to come here and disrupt my life any more than you already have." Her voice trembled with fervent anger fueled by the havoc Abigail had brought upon her world.

"Eleanor, I–"

"You may refer to me as Lady Weston," Eleanor snapped.

Abigail had been her best friend, but as she stared at the woman she had yet to invite inside, she couldn't recognize her.

"I... you're right, of course." Abigail chewed on her bottom lip. "I must apologize, Lady Weston. So much has happened, and I assure you, I never meant for any of it to unfold the way it did." She sucked in a breath. "I was young and foolish and thought I was in love." She shook her head, a flash of sadness in her eyes. "My emotions got the better of me, and I ruined a friendship I valued, as well as my reputation. But not for the reason you think."

Abigail's words caught Eleanor off guard.

"You never meant for this to happen?" Eleanor's voice wavered, thick with skepticism. "You were too caught up in your emotions?" She knew that her voice showed every hurt, every betrayal, as a raw ache, but at that moment she didn't care that Abigail saw how badly she was affected. "You knew I loved Alexander then, and now that I have married him, you want to ruin that too. Haven't you taken enough from me? What more could you possibly want? What more could I give that would finally appease you?"

A perplexed expression crossed Abigail's face. "You think I am referring to Alexander?"

Eleanor's brow furrowed deeper. "Who else could you mean?"

Abigail hesitated, a fleeting moment of uncertainty flickering across her features before she finally spoke, her voice almost a whisper. "Your father."

The room fell into a heavy silence, the weight of Abigail's words hammering into Eleanor's mind. The unexpected mention of her father, the man who raised her and who was adored by her mother, elicited a flood of conflicting emotions within her.

Eleanor's eyes widened as she sucked in a breath. The startling revelation unearthed buried memories and painful emotions she had long suppressed.

"My father..." Eleanor's voice trailed off, a tumultuous storm of emotions brewing within her.

The mention of her father opened a Pandora's Box of buried grievances, resurrecting a past that she had tried so desperately to leave behind.

Chapter Twenty-Two

Alexander immersed himself in the documents spread across his study, the steady rhythm of quill against parchment filling the room. The urgency of the task at hand consumed his focus until the abrupt entrance of a flustered servant disrupted the tranquil atmosphere.

"My lord, the woman from London is here," a breathless servant announced.

Confusion clouded Alexander's mind at the unexpected interruption until realization struck with sudden clarity.

Abigail.

The mere thought sent a jolt of apprehension coursing through him.

"Where is she?" He stood, knocking a sheaf of papers to the floor.

"They were in the music room, sir, but I believe Lady Weston took her to the drawing room and has called for tea."

Dear Lord, Abigail had accosted Eleanor in her own home? Damn the woman. Why couldn't Abigail stay away?

Abandoning his work, Alexander's pulse quickened as he hurriedly made his way out of the study, a sense of urgency propelling his steps. His mind raced with apprehension and concern, visions of the repercussions of Abigail's unannounced visit to his home flashing before him.

As he traversed the corridors, a surge of emotions gripped him—a mixture of dread, guilt, and a desperate need to rectify the situation. The image of Abigail and Eleanor engaging in conversation fueled his urgency.

Alexander reached the drawing room, his heart pounding as if he'd run from a pride of lions.

He took a moment to calm his breathing before entering the room. He darted his gaze between Abigail and Eleanor, the charged atmosphere palpable. They were both standing, their postures tense.

He approached them with measured steps, attempting to conceal the turmoil that churned within him. The weight of Eleanor's piercing gaze met his, a silent plea for explanation and reassurance amid the turmoil that had upended her life.

Sensing Eleanor's distress, Alexander closed the distance between them in swift strides, enveloping her in a tight embrace. "I'm so sorry," he murmured softly, his words a whispered reassurance amidst the chaos that surrounded them.

He released her and immediately missed the warmth of her body against his. But this needed to be dealt with. Abigail needed to be dealt with.

"What in blazes is going on here?" With his arm outstretched to keep Eleanor behind him, he glared at Abigail.

Abigail met his gaze with a resolute determination, her arms jammed across chest, spine rigid. "I have told her. There's no point in hiding it any longer."

Eleanor's gaze shifted between Alexander and Abigail, a storm of emotions flickering across her face. "My father?" Her voice wavered, cracking with a vulnerability that pierced through Alexander's heart.

Eleanor leaned back into his embrace. "I don't understand," she whispered, her voice tinged with raw pain.

As Alexander held her close, a torrent of conflicting feelings raged within him—regret, sorrow, and a heartfelt desire to shield Eleanor from the painful truths that had resurfaced.

Eleanor's tear-filled eyes gazed at Alexander, pleading for clarity amidst the whirlwind of emotions that obviously consumed her. "Please help me understand."

A heavy sigh escaped Alexander's lips, his gaze softening as he met her tearful eyes. "Let us sit. I will tell you everything."

He guided Eleanor to the sofa and directed Abigail to one of the wingback chairs. After they served tea, he dismissed the servants.

Where to start? That was the question. At the point he became involved seemed like a good idea. "I saw your father a few weeks before he died. He was at a gentleman's club, heavily intoxicated and rambling incoherently. The manager was insisting that he leave immediately due to unpaid gambling debts and threatening behavior."

He'd never forget the turmoil he witnessed in Eleanor's father during those desperate moments. "I couldn't let him return home to you and your family in such a state, so I took him home with me and helped him sober up. It was the next morning, over breakfast, that he told me everything."

Eleanor's eyes widened in surprise.

"He swore me to secrecy. In truth, I was glad to keep this secret. I didn't want to destroy the love you had for him."

A wave of conflicting sentiments washed over Eleanor—shock, disbelief, and a hint of understanding. "He struggled often, though he kept it veiled behind the façade of respectable gentleman. I knew he gambled, though I had no idea he was so indebted until I started looking after the estate."

Alexander stroked her back as she leaned into him. If only this were just about the man's gambling debts.

Amidst the charged atmosphere, Abigail's voice cut through the tension with a sense of urgency. "Alexander, I need a larger allowance. I have already explained this to you."

Alexander's brow furrowed; frustration simmered just beneath the surface. "Abigail, I will not keep giving in to your demands for more money."

"Why not? You are more than wealthy enough."

Eleanor's patience wore thin, her voice cracking with urgency. "I demand to know what's going on this instant."

Caught up in the conflict, Alexander was torn. A sense of duty and responsibility clashed with the overwhelming desire to shield Eleanor from hurt.

"Yes, Alexander, tell her." Abigail's taunting words echoed in the charged air, her persistence pushing him to the brink. "Go on, then. Tell her everything. Ruin her all over again."

Eleanor's gaze softened and she reached out, taking Alexander's hand in hers. A rush of warmth and reassurance flooded his senses. Her touch, a silent plea for trust and understanding, resonated deeply within him.

"Trust me, please. You can tell me. I just want to know the truth of what is going on. I know my father gambled away his money. I now know that he had an affair with Abigail. But why is she asking for money, and why are you paying her? Is it because the affair with Father ruined her reputation?"

With a steadying breath, he met Eleanor's gaze.

Summoning the strength, Alexander began to unravel the web of secrets that had haunted their lives. "Your father had an affair with Abigail. What you saw that fateful day years ago was me confronting Abigail when I saw her in your father's arms at the soiree."

The memory would never leave him. The shock, which had quickly turned into disbelief and then rage when Abigail used him in the way she had. He swallowed hard and continued, "When I arrived on the scene, your father disappeared into the bushes and Abigail clung to me like a limpet. I was as torn then as I am now. I couldn't call out your father without harming your relationship with him, and regardless of what I said, with Abigail obviously ravished, and with my reputation, no one would believe that I had not accosted her."

"Oh, Alexander," Eleanor murmured. "You should have told me."

"I would rather be what everyone already saw me as—a rogue—than turn your father into one."

Tears welled up in Eleanor's eyes, a mix of pain and understanding flickering within them. "You protected me." She lightly slapped his chest. "You thought you were protecting me when your deceit nearly destroyed me."

But she slumped against him, gripping his lapels in both hands.

As the burden of the truth finally lifted from his shoulders,

Alexander met Eleanor's gaze with a silent plea for forgiveness and a renewed sense of trust.

"There is more, I'm afraid." As the weight of Alexander's revelation settled heavily in the room, he continued with a sense of solemnity, "The affair produced a child, a young boy, one I'm bound by your father to care for."

Eleanor's eyes widened in disbelief. "My mother..." Her voice trailed off, the realization dawning upon her.

Alexander nodded solemnly, confirming the truth. "She knows."

Turning to face Abigail, a wave of contradictory feelings crossed Eleanor's face. "I want to meet my half-brother. Is it for him that you need the money, Abigail?"

For the first time, Abigail slumped. "I want to send him to a good school. The world will be against him as it is, so I want to make sure he has the best possible start."

Eleanor swallowed. Alexander squeezed his arm around her waist. This had to be difficult for her. "I understand. If it is just a matter of money—"

"It is not." Abigail stiffened. "You need a name to get into the best schools. The right name."

"We have discussed this, Abigail." If Alexander's jaw stiffened any more, he was pretty sure it would crack. "Attending Eton as an illegitimate son would not be easy."

"Life as an illegitimate son will not be easy," Abigail spat out.

"Why did you keep him?" Eleanor elbowed Alexander out of the way. "I mean, why not have him abroad and give him up for adoption?"

"It's what my parents wanted, and why I'm cut off from them." Abigail sighed. "I just could not do it. I held him in my arms and fell in love so deeply, I knew I couldn't let him go. I returned with him to face the ire of my parents. I went to your father to ask for his support, and he bought us a small house in Southwark and settled an annual allowance for his son's needs."

"Alexander." Eleanor stroked his arm. "Can't we do something to help? Please. It is my brother we are talking about."

"Eleanor, my love, it is not that easy..." He didn't bother finishing the sentence. Eleanor's gaze was so filled with hope, he'd find a way. He gave both ladies a nod. "I'll speak to my solicitor."

"I want to meet him. He should meet my sisters too. What have you named him, Abigail?"

"Caleb." Abigail's mouth dropped open. She stared at Eleanor with wide eyes. "Meet him?"

"Of course. He's my brother." Eleanor jutted out her chin. "I am not ashamed of him."

Confusion clouded Abigail's features as she hesitated. "I'm not sure that's a good idea. It might be better if he never meets his father's family. I've told him his father is dead."

"Well, that is the truth, isn't it? Still, he has half-sisters, and Alexander will plan for Caleb to attend Eton and then university, if he wishes."

Eleanor's quiet confidence in his ability to move mountains humbled him. But he took her hand and kissed it solemnly. His promise to her that he would look after Caleb as if he were his own was a vow sealed with the gentle touch of his lips, underscoring the depth of his commitment.

"Where is the boy now? You must have traveled to Buckinghamshire with him? Oh, my goodness. Where are you staying? Did you arrive by stagecoach today?" The questions gushed from Eleanor in a torrent of words.

Abigail still had the look of a startled animal about her. "We arrived yesterday. The innkeeper's eldest daughter is keeping an eye on him."

"Perhaps you could join us for afternoon tea today." Eleanor gave Abigail a small smile.

"I will call the carriage for you, Abigail." Alexander stood. He needed some time alone with Eleanor before they attempted a grand family get-together. "Return for lunch with Caleb. I promise, as Eleanor is prepared to attach her father's name to the child, I will do all in my power to ensure he attends the best schools. And we will keep in touch—"

"Caleb will always be welcome here," Eleanor interrupted him. "You too, Abigail. He should know his father's family."

Eleanor walked Abigail to the foyer, leaving Alexander to rake his hands through his hair and mutter a few choice curses. It seemed all his efforts to spare Eleanor the shame of an illegitimate half-brother were for naught. Had she thought through the ramifications? This could affect her sisters' debuts. Still, the boy was young enough that perhaps they could see all the sisters well settled before his identity was made public.

Eleanor returned, and his lips parted to offer an apology, but before he could utter a word, she rushed forward, enveloping him in a tight embrace.

Tears streamed down Eleanor's cheeks, her voice choked with emotion. "I thought you had—"

Before she could finish her sentence, Alexander cut in. "Never. Since I declared myself yours, you are the only woman I have ever wanted. Don't you see? I'm madly in love with you, Eleanor. I would do anything for your happiness."

Eleanor smiled, even as tears fell, and she pressed her lips against his in a tender yet impassioned kiss.

In the silent exchange of their shared embrace, the unspoken words and the depth of their emotions intertwined. The weight of the revelations and the tumultuous journey they had traversed seemed to fade away in the embrace of their love, sealing a promise of understanding, forgiveness, and an unwavering commitment to each other.

Epilogue

The carriage approached the grand estate, and Abigail's heart fluttered with nerves. She gripped her son's hand a little tighter, seeking solace in his innocent presence as they navigated the imposing gates.

Caleb jumped to his little feet when the carriage stopped, his excitement at fever pitch. She waited for the driver to help him down and then herself. Caleb, buoyed by a child's unfettered enthusiasm, bounded toward the estate's fountain, leaving Abigail to follow more cautiously.

"Mummy, the lady is naked." Giggling, he pointed at the statue of Diana surrounded by nymphs.

"She's the goddess of the Hunt, from old Roman times." Abigail took his hand and headed for the entrance.

He scuffed his feet in the gravel, kicking up a cloud of dust that did nothing to alleviate her feeling of discomfort amongst the opulence.

She couldn't help but feel out of place in this world of privilege and sophistication, a stark contrast to the life she had known recently. She'd grown up in similar surroundings, but her existence before Caleb seemed like a lifetime ago.

With each step towards the entrance, doubts gnawed at her mind.

Was this the right decision? Eleanor seemed to want to get to know Caleb, but would Alexander welcome them, or would their presence only stir further animosity and resentment?

Clutching onto a sliver of hope, Abigail steeled herself, determined to make amends and provide her son with the chance of a future unburdened by the shadows of the past. Despite the turmoil, a deep, maternal resolve fortified her spirit, reminding her that the sacrifices and the steps taken were for Caleb's future, for his chance at a life filled with opportunities she could only dream of providing alone.

Taking a deep breath to steady her nerves, Abigail lifted her chin, masking her uncertainty with composure. She rapped lightly on the knocker, her heart pounding in anticipation of what lay ahead.

The door was immediately opened by an impeccably dressed butler.

Instead of wrinkling his nose in distaste, he gave her a small nod. "Lord and Lady Weston are in the drawing room."

He took her shawl and bonnet, and with a long breath, she followed him deeper into the house. He announced her at the door to the room before moving aside so that she and Caleb could enter.

Eleanor stood to greet them. An air of tension lingered, and Abigail's heart raced with uncertainty, unsure of how Eleanor would receive her son. Her breath caught in anticipation, waiting for Eleanor's reaction.

Yet, as their eyes met, Abigail noticed a shift in Eleanor's expression. A fleeting moment of uncertainty gave way to something unexpected— a radiant smile graced Eleanor's face. Before Abigail could process the change, Eleanor stepped forward, embracing her in a warm hug, surprising her with the unexpected display of affection.

"I'm so glad you came." Eleanor's genuine warmth caught Abigail off guard.

A lump formed in her throat. She returned the embrace hesitantly, still processing the sudden turn of events.

Eleanor's attention shifted to Caleb. With an inviting smile, Eleanor crouched down to his eye level, welcoming him warmly into their home. "Hello, there! I'm Lady Eleanor." Her voice was filled with warmth and kindness. "But you can call me Auntie Ellie."

Observing Eleanor closely, Abigail noticed a gentle swell beneath her clothing—a subtle yet visible sign that Eleanor was expecting a child of her own. A surge of emotion washed over Abigail, a bittersweet mix of joy for Eleanor and a pang of longing for the family life she herself had missed.

Caleb shifted uncomfortably, no doubt shy in the unfamiliar surroundings. Abigail nudged him gently, whispering encouragingly. "Remember, good manners."

With a hesitant smile, Caleb followed his mother's cue and greeted Eleanor with a polite nod.

Eleanor's gaze lingered on Caleb, a wistful expression crossing her face. "He looks just like Father." Shaking herself out of the momentary reverie, she stood and gestured to the small sofa opposite where Alexander stood.

Caleb's curiosity seemed to override his shyness as he peeked around, taking in the grandeur of the house with wide eyes. Abigail smiled gratefully at Eleanor's warm reception, relieved by the unexpected hospitality they were receiving.

Alexander shook Caleb's hand and handed him a brightly painted Noah's Ark.

A subtle hint of suspicion lingered in Alexander's gaze. But she couldn't blame him—they had a long way to go in rebuilding trust and salvaging their relationships. Alexander's gift to Caleb, a simple yet thoughtful gesture, hinted at the potential for a thaw in the frosty relations despite the undercurrents of mistrust.

Caleb responded with a whispered thank you and a glance at his mother.

"Yes, you can play as long as you are quiet." Abigail pointed to the luxurious rug next to the sofa, and Caleb happily removed the animals from the ark.

Before they could sit and take tea, Eleanor's sisters flounced into the room. Caleb moved to her and clutched at her skirts. But it didn't take long for the girls' happiness and warmth to coax the little boy from his shell.

With a determined resolve, Abigail made a silent vow to bridge the gap that had formed between them. She knew there was much work to be done, and she was committed to restoring the harmony within their family circle.

Meanwhile, Eleanor's sisters surrounded Caleb, fussing over him with eager attention and warm smiles. Their genuine interest and kindness helped ease the boy's shyness, encouraging him to engage more openly with the family.

As they talked, drank tea, and ate delicious cakes, the atmosphere was filled with a mix of anticipation and a tentative sense of togetherness. Abigail felt a rush of emotions—gratitude for the unexpected welcome, a touch of anxiety about what lay ahead, and a sincere hope for reconciliation.

Alexander wrapped an arm around Eleanor's waist, a subtle gesture of support and solidarity.

He didn't trust her, not yet. And she knew she had a lot to make up for.

But she would.

Amidst the laughter of new connections being formed and the subtle shift towards acceptance, Abigail felt a resolve strengthen within her. This was the opportunity for a fresh start, not just for her and Caleb, but for all involved. A chance to mend what had been broken, to heal the wounds of the past, and to weave together a tapestry of a family united by more than just blood—a family redefined by love, understanding, and the courage to move beyond the shadows of yesteryears.

This comforting ambiance hinted at the possibility of a new beginning; one Abigail vowed she would not waste.